Opac

D1289136

The Wedding Audition

DEC - - 2018

The Wedding Audition

A RUNAWAY BRIDES NOVELLA

CATHERINE MANN
AND
JOANNE ROCK

TULE
PUBLISHING

The Wedding Audition
Copyright © 2015 Catherine Mann and Joanne Rock
Tule Publishing First Printing, March 2018

The Tule Publishing Group, LLC

ALL RIGHTS RESERVED

No part of this book may be used or reproduced in any manner
whatsoever without written permission except in the case of brief
quotations embodied in critical articles and reviews.

This is a work of fiction. Names, characters, places, and incidents are
products of the author's imagination or are used fictitiously. Any
resemblance to actual events, locales, organizations, or persons, living or
dead, is entirely coincidental.

ISBN: 978-1-948342-86-5

DEDICATION

In memory of DeWanna Pace, an early champion of our work and lover of quirky voices. Dee generously shared her knowledge and creativity with hungry new writers, providing much needed affirmation and guidance. We couldn't have asked for a kinder introduction to the writing world.

Chapter One

"**W**HAT'S SO WRONG with asking my guy for a threesome?"

The question blared from the radio sex talk show and fired into Annamae Jessup's mind faster than the chemicals refreshing her highlights before her rehearsal dinner tonight. Her hands clenched the armrests on the hair salon chair, the scent of the developing solution stinging her nose.

God, she could barely manage a twosome with her fiancé without breaking out into hives lately. Everyone told her it was pre-wedding jitters. She should be dancing on a cloud. She'd snagged Atlanta's golden boy, third baseman for the Atlanta Stars.

If only her engagement wasn't so public, every moment of their romance recorded by cameras because of her family's reality TV show. Thanks to the wealth of Jessup sportswear and her producer stepfather's connections, her family had become Atlanta's small time cable answer to the Kardashians – *Acting Up: The Atlanta Heiresses*.

Four years of her life had been documented since her stepfather had landed the network deal for his family. Her role? The good girl in the middle of drama while her siblings and sorority sisters partied. All she'd wanted was a peaceful life and to finish her degree in hospitality and tourism. But as a habitual family peacekeeper, she went with the flow for what the rest of them wanted, putting up with the show and hoping her part would stay small.

She wasn't the smart one or the sexy one or even the quirky one. Now the Atlanta cable area was watching the live televised special as the show's homemaker darling prepared to walk down the aisle in the ultimate love match. It was the biggest role she'd ever played on the show and she hated that it had become just that—a role.

There were even "Annamae Loves Boone" t-shirts and billboards all over town.

That's what she felt, right? Love. The nerves were to be expected. Even that radio talk show would agree.

The radio blared with the dulcet British accent as the call-in show host answered the threesome question, "It's not a matter of right or wrong, love, it's a matter of mutual consent. You and your partner need to be in agreement on your sexual journey whatever path that may take. Thank you for calling." The sound of the phone disconnecting echoed. "Next up? If you need help with your relationship, emotional or physical, call Sex Talk with Serena, that's 5-5-5-s-e-x-t-a-l-k."

Acting Up's producer, a retired game show model, waved from beside the television camera. "Turn down the radio.

We're ready to roll."

An intern scrambled to adjust the volume on "Sex Talk with Serena" to a low whisper. Darn shame. Maybe Serena could have shed some light on the cold feet setting in faster than her highlights.

Annamae pushed back a chunk of foil wraps on her hair, the black cape slick and cool against her skin heated with nerves. Celebrated stylist Lindsey Ballard wielded a comb and a paintbrush along Annamae's hair. Dressed in a Janis Joplin t-shirt and purple paisley scarf tied—pirate style— around her head, Lindsey cast meaningful looks at the junior hair designers scattered around the elite Buckhead studio. "I could use some help finishing up the color," she announced to the other stylists who'd gathered to watch her work. "Who wants to share the spotlight for fifteen minutes of fame?"

She rearranged the tail end of her purple scarf on her shoulder, fluffing the sheer fabric and winking at Annamae. Lindsey had become one of Annamae's best friends over the course of the show, winning Annamae's heart as a kindred spirit by ducking as much screen time as possible.

"I'm in." One of the interns set aside an oversized European fashion magazine he'd been thumbing through and crossed over into the camera's field, dodging an umbrella light on the way.

"Awesome." Lindsey handed the junior stylist a chunk of hair before weaving the tail end of her comb through the next section of strands, never missing a beat. "Well, what do you know? We've got a little three-way of our own going here now."

Not exactly racy stuff, but compared to Annamae's real weeknights, this afternoon's hair style three-way sounded downright exotic. "I'm settling down. I'll be a married lady by this time tomorrow."

An intimate ceremony – with a half a million of her nearest and dearest friends in TV land watching. Gulp.

"That doesn't mean the two of you can't live it up. Follow him on the road and keep those sports groupies away." Lindsey paused, dipping into the bowl of touch-up color and peering down into her friend's eyes. "Smile, Annamae, this is your big week."

Had she been frowning? Her stepfather would kill her for being "flat" on screen. She sat up straighter and tried to smile. "I'm just nervous changing my hair so close to the wedding." A good enough excuse for something she couldn't explain.

Lindsey sifted through the next batch of hair and reached for a foil. "It's not a big change. Just a little more lift than usual. You can trust me."

"I know." And she did. Lindsey wouldn't steer her wrong. "I adore your work. Your whole salon." Annamae glanced around at the wide open space filled with natural light from floor to ceiling windows. The setting sun cast pink and purple shadows on brick walls that were painted bright, shiny eggshell, decorated with framed, classic black and white photography of historic Atlanta. She'd always appreciated the way the salon gave her the necessary armor to face the cameras. Today, the place had been jazzed up for the pre-rehearsal dinner festivities with her bridesmaids, a mini-salon party for the cameras. "It's just pre-wedding jitters making me question everything."

Out of the corner of her eyes she saw the camera move closer. She could already feel the controversial statement gaining gasps from viewers. Her gut knotted at the possibility of uttering one of those sound bites that went viral and defined a person for life.

She didn't want to be that person. A doubting bride. She stared at her Medusa reflection, the foils spiking from her head like snakes.

Of course she wanted to marry Boone Sullivan. Right? Who wouldn't? He was sexy, rich, even romantic. Any commitment phobia she felt had come from issues of abandonment by her biological father. But surely she couldn't be so messed up that she would marry the wrong man just to please her stepfather?

"Every woman gets nervous before a wedding. I've got my panic attack scheduled for six days from now," Lindsey assured her over the din of nearby blow dryers while a shampoo boy escorted one of Annamae's bridesmaids toward the sinks. Lindsey was marrying a prominent Atlanta lawyer in the D.A.'s office next week, so she was no stranger to wedding hype. "But you've got nothing to be nervous about.

I was drooling over that latest tabloid photo of you and your hunky fiancé clubbing last night."

"Photo?" Did her every moment have to be documented? Silence greeted her question. Even the cameras stayed stock still as they blinked back at her with their red recording lights. "I'll have to check when I get home."

Lindsey backed up, her naturally blonde hair swishing in a low ponytail. She didn't have to fake anything with chemicals. "You don't have to wait." She pulled out her cell phone and tapped the screen to life. "Here's the whole article."

Annamae scrolled through the tabloid piece, her hands shaking. She and Boone had gone out clubbing with the second baseman from Boone's team and his new wife. At first glance they looked like two couples having fun, tearing up the town. But Annamae saw the truth in the photo. She saw love in the newlyweds' eyes. Undeniable emotion.

Annamae looked at her own face and saw ... acting. Damn good acting, but acting all the same. But was she just pretending to have fun? Or pretending to be in love?

And was the salon shrinking or were the fumes just making her dizzy?

"I'll be right back. I need to go to the ladies' room." She snatched up her purse and made fast tracks around Lindsey and another woman under a hairdryer with foils heating.

Cape flapping, Annamae raced past a line of sinks in use, past a champagne fountain and into the bathroom. She clicked on the sparkling chandelier and sagged back against the door. Her heart hammered triple time. The gilded mirror reflected scared-as-hell eyes to go with that Medusa foil wrap.

The door vibrated behind her with a pounding fist. "Annamae," her mother warbled – no doubt having downed at least three champagnes, "are you all right?"

"Fine, Mother," she gasped. "I just need a moment to catch my breath. The fumes from the chemicals are messing with my asthma."

Yet another reason she wasn't the perfect daughter. Crummy lungs. Mousy hair. And mediocre grades. She should be happy that such a charismatic man wanted to marry her, but she could only see a life of being steamrolled. Overlooked. Fading. Coming up short.

"Annamae, honey, please collect yourself quickly. We need to get those foils finished or you're going to have uneven highlights right before your wedding. Those camera lights can be particularly unforgiving."

"Of course," Annamae called back, knowing resistance was futile. Her life hadn't been her own for years, not even her hairstyle.

"Let me get your father. He can fix anything. Maybe he can talk Boone's team into giving him some downtime so you two can take a real honeymoon."

Alone. With Boone and all his perfection? Her throat closed.

"Mom, he's a baseball player. He can't just take time off

at the start of the regular season."

But her mother's voice faded and Annamae could already hear her talking into her cell phone. All of Atlanta would know what they'd planned before she would, boom microphones recording just outside the bathroom door.

Except this wasn't fake drama to keep the live wedding special interesting. This bathroom panic attack was one hundred percent genuine from her queasy stomach to her sweating forehead. No way could Mom's husband fix this.

Her stepfather was an expert at offering his children material goods in replace of the more traditional family support. In exchange for his generosity, he only expected to micromanage their social calendars, professional choices and even wardrobes. The others were younger – his biological children, still in high school and willing to be bought off in exchange for a BMW.

Wiping a mascara smear from under her eyes, she wondered how her face—only semi-attractive after last night's tears and a bout with PMS—could hide so much anger. Frustration. Fury.

Acting Up: The Atlanta Heiresses had stolen Annamae's privacy, her life, and the relationships that meant the most to her. The cameras waited.

Not seeing any hint of the good girl who'd been the moral center of her family filled with too much wealth, privilege and immaturity, she turned away from the mirror. She needed advice. Desperately. Except she couldn't think of anyone she could trust not to blast it on the show to extend their air time. Was it so wrong she'd just wanted her stepfather's attention, a father's love for the kid he'd raised for twenty-two years? She'd never truly wanted any part her producer stepfather had been pushing her toward ever since she was old enough to sing and dance with Big Bird.

She'd only signed onto this project to spend time with her parents, hopefully help her mom and step-dad through a rocky patch in their marriage. What kind of family example and hope for her own future did she have if her own core family of origin kept splitting down the middle? Well, not actual family of origin since she didn't know her real father – aka the loser alligator hunter from Alabama. He'd cut out for Australia, of all places, a month before she was born. She wanted what so few people seemed to have anymore. The picture. The family portrait kind where everyone was happy.

And she'd almost allowed that wish to push her into marrying the wrong man.

Even when she wasn't doing reality TV, cameras followed her. And all this time, she'd let them. At least on the show she didn't have to answer questions about her parents' troubled marriage, her adopted father's latest scandal or her mother's trips to rehab.

The *Acting Up* crew protected her from outside reporters while narrowing their focus to her. A questionable trade-off, she realized too late in the game.

There were two places that were off limits to the cameras.

Her bedroom.

And bathrooms.

She slid down the door to sit on the floor. The scent of roses on the sink filled the small space. She fished in her purse and pulled out her phone. Before she could think or question, she found herself dialing 5-5-5-s-e-x-t-a-l-k.

"This is Sex Talk with Serena," the lady answered with her unmistakable British accent that had made her a sensation on the American radio waves. "Whom am I speaking to and what can I help you with, love?"

"Uhm, this is ... Annam—er—." She stopped herself. "Anna. And I need your help with advice in the romance department."

"Well, Anna, I'll do my best."

She struggled for the right words to sum up her situation, currently more tangled than her hair. "I'm engaged to be married and it's a fairy tale match."

"That sounds amazing. But clearly you don't agree or you wouldn't be phoning. What's the catch?"

"I feel like it's just a fantasy. How do I know if I really love this man?" Annamae didn't know who was making her mouth move, because she never spoke out of turn, conscious all her life of being viewed as overprivileged and working hard to overcome the image.

A sympathetic sigh filled the receiver. "I can't answer that for you. But I can say if you have any doubts at all, you need to postpone the wedding. A marriage is supposed to be forever."

"But he's going to be hurt and we'll both be embarrassed." Publically. Horribly.

"Hurt. Embarrassed. I notice you didn't say brokenhearted," she pointed out aptly. "Truly, it's only going to hurt worse if you break up after the vows are spoken."

God, the truth was easy. The actions were tough.

"You're saying I have to call it off?" Her knees stopped shaking for a second, as if her body recognized the truth before her brain did. She repeated the words, wondering if she could force herself to do the impossible, "I have to call it off."

The knocking on the door resumed, a light tapping this time.

"Annamae?" the hairdresser, her friend, Lindsey, called softly.

She put the phone on mute. "Thanks. I'm almost done. I'll be right out so you can finish my hair."

"Annamae," Lindsey whispered, "uh, the radio is on out here and everyone knows it's you on the call-in show. You just broke up with your fiancé on the reality show via the radio. Live."

Horror sucker punched all the air from her lungs. Annamae stared down at the phone cradled in her lap. Had she really just done that?

Panic made her chest go tighter, sending her hand groping in her pocket for her inhaler as she thought of her words heard by so many. All those people. Her parents.

And Boone.

Oh God. She closed her eyes tight as her world tipped sideways. She couldn't go back out there and face the cameras. She couldn't face her fiancé who deserved so much better than a halfway committed bride who may or may not have just done this awful thing accidentally on purpose in a massive passive-aggressive way.

Already she could hear the volume increasing outside the door. Her mother's shriek. The producer shouting. Dozens of cell phones ringing in unison like some kind of flash mob prank.

She needed to get away from here and arrange a time to talk to Boone. Privately, and please Lord, maybe before he heard. But first and foremost, she had to get away from the media or things would be worse. Far worse.

Scrambling to her feet, she jammed her phone in her back pocket. The pressure of being followed night and day finally exploded, her world narrowed to one thought. Escape and regroup. And there was only one person who'd apparently never bought into her lifestyle. One relative who had never shown up in town for a chance to be on the show. The same person her mother and stepfather did their best to keep out of her life.

Her paternal grandmother. The woman who'd given birth to the loser alligator hunter. Maybe a dose of reality—real freaking reality and not the made for TV variety—could help her understand herself. Her past. Her future.

She just needed a few days to get her bearings and a retirement home in a rural Alabama town might well be the only place she could find that space.

And the risk of being recognized or tracked? She would have to move fast. Empty her account. Buy a cheap used car with cash from a private seller. Make some simple adjustments to her appearance. The cable show was popular, but the reach wasn't that huge. They hadn't been syndicated, despite her stepfather's best efforts.

Mind made up, she tugged foils out of her hair, throwing them in the trash as she cranked on the water. Sticking her head under the faucet, she washed out the chemicals, using some of the liquid hand soap for a quick lather. She squeezed out the excess water then flipped back her shoulder length hair, shaking it loose.

Almost done. She eyed the window, then looked back at the door practically vibrating from all the people knocking on it. She tugged her shirt from the hanger and stuffed it in her purse. There wasn't time to change out of the cape now.

She closed the toilet seat lid and climbed on top to reach the window and crank it open. She hefted up, water slipping under the neck of the cape and down her spine. Muscles screaming, she shimmied through, wobbling for a moment before the grabbed a tree and tugged herself out of the building.

For a surreal moment, she hung by her arms, legs swinging, the narrow alley below her deserted for now. Other than a scruffy little mutt staring back up at her, wide eyes in a scrawny body. Her feet hit the gravel hard and the dog yipped.

"Shhhh!" Annamae pleaded. "They'll hear you. Scoot. Okay, fella? Or girl. Or whatever. Go home."

Although it didn't look like it had a home. The dog lifted a leg and peed on an overturned trashcan. Definitely a boy. He cast a forlorn look at all the newspapers in the trash. A million words of caution shouted through her head about not picking up strays and what if the dog didn't have vaccinations—not that he appeared particularly rabid. Just hungry.

She looked left and right. Her car was a quick sprint away where she always hid it to bypass the mob and enter privately. But the dog. She opened her purse and pulled out the remaining half of her bagel she hadn't been able to choke down and passed it to the dog.

"I really gotta go, little guy." She glanced over her shoulder at the window that would soon be filled with camera lenses. The scraggly mutt cocked his head to the side, bagel in his mouth and it broke her heart to leave him, but she couldn't spare another second.

Black cape flapping as she ran, she clutched her purse to her stomach. The dog ran after her. And caught up. Tiny paws triple timed to keep pace alongside her, the onion bagel still in his mouth. Maybe she didn't have to leave him behind after all. She sure as hell could use a friend to keep her company on the trip ahead.

Because as soon as she got some cash and a different set of wheels, she would leave this disaster of a life in the dust. She was Alabama bound.

GOD, HE COULDN'T wait to leave Alabama behind.

Drying his face with a kitchen towel, Wynn Rafferty – known around these parts as Heath Lambert – crossed off another day on the John Deere calendar tacked above the breadbox.

Another day closer to the trial. Another day still breathing. And if he wanted it to stay that way, he had to keep a very low profile here until that drug lord's trial in Miami set Wynn's life back on track again.

He tossed aside the pen and the towel, a yellow tiger-striped cat streaking past him on the countertop before he chased her off. Or was that one a him? Damned if he remembered. He'd started feeding one feral cat and suddenly he had six. He'd have to make another call to the vet to schedule a checkup for the new arrival. Although the clipped ear indicated someone had already spayed or neutered ... Tiger. He would call him/her Tiger.

He pulled open the fridge for milk to offer the questionably gendered cat and grabbed himself a beer. It was early in the day for a long neck—just past noon—but he'd done the work of five men since rising at dawn to beat the heat of another Alabama scorcher. He'd never cut it as a fruit grower long-term, but the last year since he'd purchased the small orchard had taught him he needed to be disciplined if he wanted anything to show for his efforts. The work Wynn did in his former life had demanded intense focus and commitment, but even undercover work hadn't been as physically grueling as his stint in the orchard peppered with a few pecan trees.

He poured milk for the ragtag bunch of cats who were his main source of company these days. Popping the top on his beer, Wynn stood in front of the calendar emblazoned with a John Deere 1943 Serial H tractor and stared at the days leading up to the trial that would demand his return to Miami under armed escort. Until then, he was stuck in this low-key witness protection program under an assumed name. He was tired as hell of being "Heath Lambert."

Part of him couldn't wait to put the whole ordeal behind him so he could move on, but another voice in his head dreaded going back and facing the memories of the undercover operation that had gone sour, allowing the Dimitri crime family to destroy key evidence while an innocent teen had been caught in the crossfire.

Old resentments burned his throat in ways the dark lager couldn't begin to quench. He scratched the head of the nearest cat, an animal who looked as though it had been through the same kind of year as him—one ear chewed and a patch of missing fur the vet said was from an old fight. But Patchy looked ready for battle just the same. Wynn hoped he'd bounce back just as tough.

The intercom system on his security module beeped and he shook off the memories. His setup wasn't super high tech because of the low threat level in a town like Beulah, Alabama, but he did have two hidden cameras on the only entrance into the property.

The feed on a fourteen-inch screen near the security controls showed a vintage Volkswagen Beetle convertible, cherry red, top down with a woman and a scruffy dog inside. The dog rode shot gun, paws shooting up to rest on the top of the door now that the car had stopped. As for the woman, she wore a dotted scarf that covered most of her hair. A few white blonde locks slipped free. Big sunglasses hid most of her face, but her full, pouty lips pursed for a moment before she spoke into the intercom.

"My name is Annamae and this is my new friend, Bagel." She pointed to the dog. "We're interested in renting the carriage house." She tipped her head to the side. Her car might be a rattletrap and her clothes thrift store quality, but she had an air about her, something that was too expensive for Beulah. But she didn't look like the type to associate with deadly Miami street gangs either. Definitely more wholesome and a little uptight, born to wealth and privilege in spite of her old school VW in need of a serious tune-up.

"What do you know about the carriage house?" He released the talk button.

He hadn't advertised the property the former owner rented out because anonymity equaled security. Something he wouldn't have if he allowed a tenant access to his grounds.

"That's a peculiar question." She tapped her chin, her eyebrows slanting down in an expression that brought a little storm cloud over Snow White's perfect face. "If I knew much about it, I wouldn't want to see it."

He noticed how carefully she rearranged the pooch on her front seat, steering it away from the door and patting its head. Two seconds later, the mutt jumped to put both front paws on the door again, furball yapping at the intercom, tail wagging like crazy.

His thumb circled around the talk button while he considered whether or not to let her in. He had to admit he wouldn't mind the extra income during his forced time away from his job on the police force. Especially if his apple crop turned out as crappy as he feared. He'd thought farming would keep his mind off his past. He hadn't considered he might have a serious black thumb.

All financial concerns aside though, if she was a gangster intent on getting inside to kill him, she'd probably make more of an effort to sweet talk him, wouldn't she? And even if she was a badass hitwoman in the world's worst getaway car, he needed to know that as well.

Bottom line, making too big a deal out of being a hermit

would call more attention to himself. So he pressed the button to open the gate for Ms. Uptight with the happy mutt... What was its name? Baggy? Badger? Bagel?

Still, he rechecked his weapon at his side before "Heath Lambert" went out to greet her, knowing only dead men took chances on innocent-looking faces.

Chapter Two

"DON'T WORRY, BAGEL. It's going to be fine." An-namae talked to her new pet under her breath as she steered her recently purchased VW Beetle into the Fort Knox of Beulah, Alabama, population twenty-two rednecks and thirty-seven dogs.

Or so it seemed.

She'd acquired *her* dog much sooner in her journey. Her escape out of Atlanta had been nerve-wracking and she'd been grateful she had Bagel to keep her company – well, as much as he could keep her company in between downing hamburgers. She'd been afraid he would make himself car sick, but so far he'd just belched and tucked his nose into the wind. She'd taken a risk and put on large glasses to stop at the Walgreens mobile vet to get him a rabies vaccination, then hit the road again, feeling quite proud of herself for being so detail oriented. Poor pup.

As if to say he wasn't worried in the least, Bagel barked and wagged his tail. His fur had a wiry, terrier quality to it, the chocolate chip cookie coloring a blend of cream with darker patches. He seemed like a very upbeat dog, not that she knew much of anything about animal temperament. Her stepdad had been allergic to everything with fur, except her mother's mink coat. Yet so far, the dog hadn't bothered her asthma a bit.

She steered around a pothole that Bagel would have gotten lost in. "No matter what the so-called carriage house looks like, it's got to be better than what we've seen."

Her day of house hunting hadn't uncovered anything remotely suitable, even for an Atlanta girl trying hard not to turn up her nose at real estate with no skyline views. She'd chosen Beulah for its remote location, after all, so she couldn't very well complain. Beulah also happened to be the town where her biological father had grown up and the present home of Annamae's still-living grandmother, a fact that had blown her away when her mother let it slip that her grandmother was still alive.

Delilah Jessup, queen of parties and limelight, had hidden her ex-lover's roots for as long as Annamae could remember, writing off Annamae's grandmother as a strictly religious person who'd disowned her son for impregnating Delilah. Then, she'd rejected the baby. For years, Annamae had accepted her mother's word on that, even believed that the old woman had passed away. But now that she knew her grandmother was alive this seemed the perfect time to dig around for more about her roots. To find out who she really was, who her father was, so she could finally have a relationship she didn't self-destruct.

Maybe that would be the one blessing that came out of the latest mess *Acting Up* had made of her life. And of Boone's. God, she felt the worst for him.

She'd called her fiancé – *ex*-fiancé – to have him meet her at a coffee shop so she could break up with him face to face, but he hadn't answered. He'd texted her that her radio chat had already gone viral. There was nothing more to be said and that if she were wise she would stay away from him and out of the shit storm she'd stirred up in Atlanta.

Then nothing else. Just like that. The man who'd said he loved her more than life itself wouldn't answer her calls. Wouldn't talk. They'd resorted to text messages. He'd accused her of using the wedding—and the break-up—as a way to drive up ratings.

That hurt, but she couldn't blame him for thinking as much. She deserved that and worse for what she'd done.

She'd chickened out at that point and opted to send texts to her mother and father asking them to respect her privacy and give her some time, then turned off her phone altogether before they could track her. Which they would.

Right now, driving through a half mile of stumpy trees over a pitted gravel road, she just wanted time to process the fact that tomorrow she was not going to become Mrs. Boone Sullivan. They were no longer in love. She'd come so close to making the worst mistake of her life. The Atlanta media were already having a field day eating her alive over dumping their Golden Boy on a radio show, no less. They were calling her the Hit and Run Bride.

Who would have thought her voice would be so easily identifiable as Anna on the radio? She'd tried to talk softly and disguise herself. Unlike her half-sisters, she was the quiet good girl. They were the ones that grabbed the headlines with scandal.

Once she found peace with her past, then she'd start a future of her own. Whatever that life might entail – something else she had to figure out.

She pulled her head out of old problems while taking the potholes slowly on her way up the sloping drive. She had plenty of new complications to focus on, like how to introduce herself to a grandmother who didn't want anything to do with her. Or where to lay her head tonight since the town's one "motor inn" was *not* an option. They didn't allow dogs for one thing. She would sleep in her new-used car before she returned to the Sleep Tight Motor Lodge and the scent of Lysol so strong, her eyes were still watering after a brief trip inside.

In the lobby, she'd overheard locals talking about the reclusive new farmer in town and his carriage house for rent. Reclusive landlord sounded perfect to her. She'd gotten directions from the local gas station, and here she was.

She spotted the ramshackle farmhouse and its alleged owner at the same time she cleared a gatehouse, a few barns and what looked to be a tractor graveyard full of rusty metal beasts. The massive farmhouse was probably charming at one time, its clapboard siding still bright white despite a few spots of peeling paint. Pecan trees sprawled in the front yard with heavy limbs in need of tending. Empty window boxes would have cheered the place considerably if anyone had taken time to plant trailing roses or even a few geraniums.

An iron pump in the side yard near a well was bracketed by some kind of fruit trees that looked as badly in need of tending as everything else. Three more years and the place would be a dump. But right now, it still looked salvageable to a woman who'd just contemplated spending a night in a bed that included a coin-operated massage feature.

The man sauntering toward her while she parked her car, on the other hand, didn't look as if he'd *ever* been charming. A guy with a build like that would have been a shoo-in for security on the show… exactly the type of broad shoulders she liked to hide behind in big crowds. Looking at him, Annamae realized in a skipped heartbeat why there weren't flowers. Any man whose shirt was sweaty by noon and who scowled forbiddingly at potential tenants—even a potential tenant with a great deal of practice at making men smile from her years when she was still her father's trained per-former—didn't understand anything about the value of appearances.

Although, she had to admit that his appearance, while daunting, had a definite appeal. His wide shoulders and tightly cropped hair gave him an action hero, Jason Statham vibe. He had that tough-dude thing going even though he was shadowed at ten paces by a huge yellow cat with half an ear missing. Something about the tough man with a tough cat made her smile.

Bagel also appeared keen to make acquaintances, barking merrily at the pair until the cat raced toward the car like it might tear him limb from limb. Annamae thought she'd better leave the dog just in case.

"You look familiar." The man stalking closer didn't seem to note the animal mini-drama. He stopped three feet away from the bright red Beetle and stared, making no attempt to open her car door.

Every southern man she'd met in this slow-as-molasses state had played the gentleman for her since her arrival. Even the tobacco-spitting old guy who ran the Sleep Tight Motor Lodge had scurried to hold doors for her, and he obviously hadn't stirred himself to clean his hotel's rooms since the nineteen seventies. "Everybody says I look like that girl on the Vampire series. Guess we all have doppelgangers. About your cabin…?"

"Try the Sleep Tight Motor Lodge."

Not even a sorry, ma'am? Or an offer of directions?

She was a Southerner from birth, but big city Atlanta southern, which was a far reach from Beulah, Alabama. She tried to place his accent. More of a non-accent with only a hint of southernese.

Some folks thought all southern accents sounded the same. She fought that stereotype on TV all the time with guests they brought onto the reality show. The fake, generic southern accent was like fingernails on a chalkboard to her. And this guy's accent wasn't Alabama southern. He couldn't fool her with that Roll Tide t-shirt.

He wasn't Georgia southern either. She needed a little more conversation to nail down his roots.

"You're not from around here, are you?" She reached outside to grab the handle since the door wouldn't open from the inside. But she had to watch her money and this car had been a bargain. It didn't run like her Beemer, but her strawberry-mobile had a charm of its own. She swung her legs around to the dirt driveway, reminding Bagel to stay put so he wouldn't be eaten by any psycho cats.

Her host's eyes drifted downward, taking in her wrinkled yellow sundress, the hem inching up over her knee as she rose. He might not be southern, but he was still very much a man.

"I moved to Beulah because I like it quiet. Very quiet," the man returned, offering her his hand. "Heath Lambert."

"Anna Smith." She gave over her fingers to his grip, encouraged he hadn't displayed any concrete recognition at her semi-famous face so far. A good thing. The sunglasses and clothes were new from Walmart. Her hair was worse than a Medusa horror because the highlights hadn't been finished right, unevenly placed and some nearly white. But she was scared to put coloring on it right away for fear her hair would fall out. For now she opted for a scarf to keep from drawing too much attention to herself.

Not that she gave a rat's patootie about her appearance today. She'd been engaged only a few hours ago, ready to pledge her life to another man. In love. Sorta.

The touch of this guy's hands—sun-warmed and hard-working—shot an unexpected jolt through her. A damn unwelcome jolt. She didn't like what it said about her that she could be attracted to someone else the day before her wedding.

Her called-off wedding.

Besides, Heath Lambert wasn't at all her type with his suspicious expression and dark eyes that held too many secrets for an apple grower. But he was attractive enough, other than being the dangerous type.

Her therapist called them self-destruct guys, meaning women who let themselves get involved with them would self-destruct in a matter of months. Something all of Atlanta knew too since her sessions had been part of the show. Did therapy really count if it wasn't private? The counselor hadn't liked that question when she'd raised it, steering the conversation back to her. Annamae had plenty of vices, but thankfully, swooning over bad boys wasn't one of them.

Not before, anyway, and she couldn't afford to change that pattern now.

"Smith." His hand fell away as he looked her over. "That a local name?"

"Actually, yes. My grandmother is in the retirement center complex behind your orchard and I moved to town to be closer to her." It was sort of the truth. A little of the truth.

Annamae had considered herself a Jessup as soon as her mother married her stepfather. But in Beulah, she'd been using her birth father's last name even though he'd never married her mom. She prayed with a new hair color and a few other changes to her appearance, the town in general wouldn't recognize her from the show, not that they knew about her connection to Granny Smith.

Granny Smith?

She frowned, looking at the apple orchard.

"How did you find out about the carriage house over there?" He tipped his head toward a clump of buildings to the right of the main house.

"The man who runs the service station across from the Sleep Tight Motor Lodge gave me directions. Gus Fields." She perched a hand on her hip. "So is it for rent or not?"

He gave a clipped nod. "This way. But fair warning, it's nothing fancy."

"I'm not picky." Which technically wasn't true. She didn't like her food mixed on her plate. She always slept with three pillows at night. And apparently she was very choosy about marriage.

Maybe she needed to stop playing the good girl role if she was going to figure out who she really was during this trip.

She followed Heath up the driveway toward the buildings he'd indicated. They passed a tiny brick structure that might have been a pump house or a smokehouse where she spotted a lounging calico cat on the roof. A weathered gray barn even bigger than the main house loomed to her left. Behind that she spied a two-story carriage house with antique doors that swung open on hinges instead of lifting up like a traditional garage. Like everything else on Lambert's property, the carriage house needed a new coat of paint and some refurbishing, but she could tell at a glance the place had potential. For the first time since she'd decided to come to Beulah, she wondered if life in her self-imposed lay-low time in rural Alabama might hold a few pleasant surprises.

He unlocked a side entrance and pushed open a squeaking door. A gray cat darted out like a startled ghost. She wouldn't have expected a cranky man living alone to be a keeper of so many cats. "I haven't decided if I'm going to rent it out although I hear the past few owners have."

Disappointment stung. Bad. She really wanted this place, with an intensity that surprised her. It was rural in a way she'd never experienced before, making her want to take a deep breath for the first time in ages. No feelings of a tight-chested, impending asthma attack. She liked knowing there were no cameras lurking nearby. That she could turn a cartwheel out on the lawn and it wouldn't ever be captured on film. Plus, in spite of her decidedly grouchy host, the place had the potential to be charming.

Although he didn't turn on a light switch, Annamae liked what she saw in the shadowy interior. Somebody had done a nice job of converting the space, paying careful attention to maintaining the character of the exterior stone walls while still creating a functional living area. A lot better than anything else this town had to offer. Beulah wasn't much of a condo town and she was still working off cash for now so buying a place was out of the question.

Renting for a month or two until interest in her too public breakup died down meant she'd either be sharing a moth-eaten old home with a nosy widow or convincing Heath Lambert to let her stay here. Amid all this remote privacy. With his security system to ensure no one found her.

It was meant to be.

She followed her silent host through the rooms in the dark, her eyes adjusting to the low light filtering in through closed blinds and shutters the longer they remained indoors. When they returned to the living area, she couldn't stand the quiet any longer.

"I don't know why you wouldn't want to rent it. I wouldn't ask you to make any changes to the property." Annamae figured money would smooth the way, especially since the whole place looked like it hadn't seen an influx of funds in a long time. "I can pay cash for the first month, last month and security."

No easy feat considering she'd just left her job as a reality show actress and applying for a new job would reveal her identity to the locals and defeat the whole purpose of hiding out. She waited for the surly owner to answer her, but he only stared back at her, scowling.

"Mr. Lambert? How much?"

"I haven't decided what to charge." He picked up a corner of one of the dusty furniture coverings and peered underneath it as if he had no idea what he'd find.

"Whatever number you're thinking of, add two or three hundred more." She waved her pink leather wallet ever so slightly for emphasis. "I'm not opposed to paying extra security if it will make your decision easier."

And faster. Memories of Lysol and a vibrating bed ensured she'd pay this man whatever her wallet contained. She could already see herself at home here, opening the blinds and napping in the sunshine in a way that she never could at home. Open blinds only invited long-range zoom lenses.

His dark eyes lingered on her in the shadowy room, making her wonder if she should have found a real estate agent to escort her around town for safety purposes more than anything. She wasn't as vulnerable as she looked since she traveled with a few specially made safety devices given to her by one of the show's security guards, but those gizmos would only help so much against a man of Heath's size. In a remote area far from town.

She didn't think Bagel would be much help if he'd been cowed by a tiger-striped cat missing part of his ear.

Just when she was about to dig in her purse for her can

of mace, Heath's intense scrutiny of her person ended and he reached for the door.

"I'd have to do a background check on you if you're serious about moving in." He held the door for her as she walked past him into the bright sunlight of midafternoon. "Would that present a problem?"

She nearly tripped over her own feet, before walking again, her feet clicking along pecans littering the walkway.

"Background check? Uhm, I have a vaccination record for my dog. Straight from the E-z Mobile Vet Clinic right outside of Walgreens. Good people get their pets vaccinated." She cast a sideways glance hoping to distract him since he was clearly a fan of animals. "Your cats are vaccinated. Right?"

Who knew what he'd find out about Anna Smith, a name that might be shared by hundreds? She couldn't give him her real name. Then all of Beulah would know about the embarrassing, heartless way she'd dumped Atlanta's most beloved player.

"Yes, my cats are vaccinated, spayed and neutered – unlike your dog, by the way." He pointed out as Bagel lifted a leg and showed off his boy skills as he watered a tree. Heath halted near the big barn on their way back toward her car. "And yes, I need the background check. I'd never give somebody keys to the gate out front without making sure there's not a criminal record or bad credit report."

He studied her closely, as if he could see past the good

girl exterior to her terribly wayward character beneath.

"Sure. No problem." She would brazen it out and see what happened. Maybe Anna Smith would come up clean. Or better still, maybe her would-be landlord was just bluffing to see if she gave anything away. What backwoods Alabama farmer did background checks anyway?

Liking this theory tremendously, she stuffed her wallet back in her purse and fished for a pen instead. She would fill out whatever paperwork he produced.

His beeper went off before she could flick her Bic in his face. He reached for the device attached to his belt, which she decided didn't look quite like a beeper after all.

"There's somebody at my gate." Frowning, he pressed a button that must have been wired to the same intercom system she'd used when she arrived. "Yes?"

"Mr. Lambert? This is Gus from down at the service station. Did a young lady happen to stop by yet today? She was looking for a place to rent."

A bad feeling tickled her spine as Heath glanced her way.

"Actually, I'd rather you not spread the word that I have a place, Gus. I haven't decided if I want to rent it out." He paused, staring at her, and for a moment Annamae thought she was off the hook. But then he clicked the talk button on the radio device. "And the woman is here now."

A chorus of other voices could be heard behind Gus when he came over the intercom again. Oh God. She'd been careful. So careful.

"Well damnation, Mr. Lambert, your guest is a bon-a-fide celebrity." He stretched the phrase out into exaggerated syllables.

Apparently not careful enough. How long before her parents showed up? She felt sick to her stomach.

Gus continued while Heath scowled, "Do you mind if I bring a few friends around to meet the *Acting Up* star who just dumped her baseball playin' fiancé on the radio, no less? I brought along some folks who are long-time fans of Annamae Jessup and her TV show."

Heath didn't bother to answer. He shook his head and clipped the intercom radio back on his belt.

"Anna Smith was it?" His hard eyes glittered with passing judgment. "I think you'd better take your fans and be on your way, Ms. *Jessup*."

"They're not my fans." She gulped. Swallowed. Hoped he didn't throw her to the dogs. That is, the lovely people gathered at his front entrance. If they snagged a photo of her, it would be all over the Internet before she could sneeze out *gone viral*. "I mean, there's been some mistake."

"I'm sure. But I prefer my privacy." He turned on his heel and stalked back toward her car.

Panicking, she wondered how to salvage this mess. How she could convince Heath she would be a quiet, excellent tenant. Maybe a tactical retreat was in order. She could go find her grandmother and think about a Plan B. Because she was determined to stay here, in this fortress of an apple orchard. She would live off stolen fruit and a handful of shelled pecans if she had to. No one would get inside those gates. She felt at peace here—for at least a little while—in a way she couldn't remember feeling in a long time.

"Maybe you could think about it overnight," she suggested, stopping short as they neared her convertible VW Bug. "Oh, look at them!"

Bagel lay on the hood of the VW convertible Bug. Beside him, the half-eared cat lounged, tail swishing like a whip while it glared out at the world with hooded eyes. Bagel's tail thumped the hood as he spied her, his ears standing up straight.

Without a word, Heath strode over to his cat and plucked it from the hood, sending it off toward the smokehouse with a nudge.

"Goodbye, Ms. Smith-Jessup." He leaned against a huge rusty plow and propped an elbow on the machinery, waiting for her to leave.

She chewed her lip.

"Isn't there a back way out of here?" She peered around the property, noticing the road she'd driven in on continued in two different directions behind the house. "I'd love to… er… protect your privacy by causing as little disturbance as possible."

"Won't your fans be disappointed?" He glowered at her.

He excelled at glowering. Annamae thought he would make a convincing TV villain. Female fans would swoon over him, even if he was the opposite of hero-material Boone Sullivan in every way.

"They're mistaken, remember?" She picked up Bagel and snuggled her new pet before settling him back onto the front seat of her car. "I'd appreciate it if you'd let your friends know the next time you see them."

He growled out a frustrated breath. "I've got a camera on a back gate." He pointed toward the road that led left. "Head that way and when I see you reach the gate, I'll open it. Briefly. I suggest you drive out as fast as possible."

Definite villain material. She smiled brightly, calling on all her good girl charm, honed on camera for so long she hardly knew who she was underneath the act.

"Of course." She scribbled down the number for a pre-paid cell phone on a piece of paper and handed it to him. "Please let me know if you change your mind about the rental. I'm going to visit my grandmother, but I'd love to hear from you anytime."

And while he was thinking, she would be figuring out how to work her way into that carriage house.

He took the paper and shoved it in the pocket of his jeans.

"Off to grandmother's house." His lips stretched in a way that was more snarl than smile. "I hear the woods are full of wolves, Red. Be careful."

Red? She patted her polka dot crimson head scarf self-consciously, a move that made him smile for real. Forgetting all about her effort to charm him, she hit the gas and drove off, away from Heath Lambert and all his surly smugness.

She would convince him to rent that place to her, one way or another. She'd dealt with tougher wolves than him surviving in her father's world.

WYNN IGNORED HIS ringing phone a few hours after his unwanted guest's departure. It had been easy enough to track her identity online as soon as he'd typed in Annamae... the search suggestions practically begged him to search for Annamae Jessup, who'd just made headlines back in Atlanta by jilting one of baseball's best athletes. Why did a TV personality have to show up in the town he'd studied backward and forward to ensure a quiet, anonymous existence?

Not exactly what he was looking for when he'd moved here a year ago after his investigation of a street gang had exploded. After his identity was compromised, U.S. Marshalls had encouraged him to get out of the city and into a safe house until the trial to protect his testimony, but Wynn refused to soak off the system long term. Bad enough he had to take an enforced leave from the city's police force. He would go stir crazy in a tiny hotel room for months on end. This seemed a stronger cover and wiser hideout.

Until now.

He might not have a choice if his enemies saw *his* picture in a newspaper thanks to Annamae's presence in Alabama. He used a different name now, but he hadn't done much to change his appearance besides shave off a beard since Beulah was so small. Remote.

The trial started in three weeks. Surely he could weather that time here. But a part of him had begun to wonder if he'd been foolish to let Annamae leave. At least on his property, he could keep an eye on her. Because what if he'd somehow compromised her safety?

The thought chilled him.

Plus, if she truly wanted privacy—a fact underscored by the way she'd sneaked out the back gate—he could provide that here. Annamae Jessup could all but disappear on this property, surrounded by fences and cameras to keep out unwanted guests. If she remained in Beulah somewhere else, she'd only serve as a beacon for national media interest. And that would not be good for anyone.

He had enough supplies within the confines of his fenced orchards that he could probably remain locked inside the perimeter until the U.S. Marshals Service arrived via helicopter to take him back home. Back to Miami where his testimony could ensure key members of a particularly vicious street gang would live out their days behind bars.

He couldn't let Atlanta's runaway heiress jeopardize everything he'd worked so hard to accomplish. He'd have to find her and help her be as invisible to the world as he'd become—at least for three more weeks.

"Beulah Retirement Community"

The sign tilted to the side, half-buried in kudzu less than a mile from Heath Lambert's farmhouse. She was finally here. At Grandma's house.

Gulp.

Nerves tap danced overtime in her stomach. Surely that was just because of the whole debacle of her wedding and the worst hide out attempt. Ever.

Heath had helped her slip out a back gate, but she'd still felt like spiders were crawling all over her, her skin burning with the sense of being watched. She'd checked her rearview mirror compulsively, but only saw normal traffic. She was just being paranoid. This wasn't Atlanta.

Annamae stepped out of her car and walked up the flag-stone path to the three-story Victorian that looked like new construction despite the old-fashioned appeal. By all accounts her grandmother—Hazel Mae Smith—lived here at the retirement center, referred to as the old folks' home by the gas station attendant earlier. He'd apologized if that sounded politically incorrect to a big city girl but around here they didn't believe changing words changed reality.

Did she really want to meet Hazel Mae, a woman Annamae's mother hadn't bothered to call in twenty-some years and labeled dead? When confronted after her slip up, Delilah Jessup had written off the rift with Hazel Mae as "old baggage" as if that somehow alleviated the need for Annamae to concern herself with her grandmother's presence in the world. But as far as Annamae could see, wasn't that all the more reason to fix the problem? What old baggage could possibly prove important enough to keep Annamae from seeing her only living grandparent for that long?

Sure Annamae had wanted to write off her own parents a time or two when their public disputes turned their lives into a media circus, but she'd always hung on to the philosophy that family was worth the extra effort.

Decision made, Annamae charged up the steps to the porch with her dog tucked under her arm. She turned the low door handle favored by old people and arthritic fingers, more bar than knob. A few kids played in the foyer with crayons and paper near a polished wooden toy box with an elephant painted on the front. A lady who was probably their mother sat in a rocking chair beside a frail-looking old man who frowned and stared at a television as if the thought of visiting with relatives was a wholly unwelcome idea. The kids' eyes lit up at the sight of the dog.

Gramps looked up. "Your dog's not wearing a vest."

Annamae paused. "Pardon me?"

Grumpy Gramps pointed to Bagel. "Your dog ain't wearing a therapy dog vest. He can't go inside to visit with the residents. Rules are the rules for the pets that come here."

His eyes narrowed. "You ain't one of those people who tries to pass off fake working dogs just so you can carry your pet in your purse are ya?"

She blinked fast at the crash course on working dogs 101. "Uhm, no sir. I just can't leave my dog in the car and I'm here to see someone and—."

He plucked the pooch from her arms. "I'll hold him outside 'til you're done. And don't worry about me wandering off with him. My daughter here watches me like a hawk since I snuck out for a beer last month. Before you know it, she'll be making me wear one of those ankle monitors like I'm some kind of criminal instead of the man who taught her to tie her shoes."

Annamae looked from the older man to the daughter who nodded with obvious gratitude over having found something that made her father happy.

"Sure," Annamae said. "Thank you for holding my dog, sir. I appreciate it. His name is Bagel."

His gnarled hands stroked Bagel's bristly fur. "Just don't take too long. I'm not a dog sitter."

"Of course. I'll be as quick as I can."

The daughter mouthed *thank you* as Annamae grasped the handle again and backed inside.

Beyond the reception area, a brightly lit check-in desk was bracketed by two thriving fichus trees in front of a curving staircase to a second floor. An elevator chimed somewhere in the background, suggesting the stairs were probably more for show. The Persian carpet runner down the middle certainly looked brand new.

"Can I help you, ma'am?" A young, dark-haired woman in hospital scrubs sat behind the desk, a diet soda at her elbow.

Annamae tugged the knot in her scarf tighter. "I'm looking for a resident. Hazel Mae Smith."

Hopefully her grandmother didn't share the disposition of the man in the reception area more interested in his crossword puzzle than the toddler waving a crayon drawing under his nose.

"Certainly. May I tell her who's calling, Ms. Jessup?" The desk attendant – Bobbi, according to the nametag decorated with teddy bears in nursing hats – grinned as she picked up her cell phone.

Annamae ducked behind a fichus tree, staring at the cell phone in horror. "No photos. Seriously. Or I'll contact your boss."

Bobbi gasped. "I wouldn't dare take a photo. I was just going to show you the story on the Internet so you could be careful."

"Surely you understand why I'm wary of trusting you." Annamae leaned back against the wall, but wasn't ready to step out of hiding yet.

"Honey, I let my mama push me into marrying my high school sweetheart and he turned out to be a total jackass – pardon my language. He expected me to wait on him hand

and foot all the time, then ran off with my best friend."

Annamae inched out from behind the tree. If the young woman wanted to take a photo, a measly fake tree wasn't going to stop her. "I'm sorry to hear that."

"Me too," Bobbi said, straightening the nametag on her surgical scrub. "I like my job and all, but I lost four years of my life and all my savings. It's better to be sure."

Stepping forward, Annamae swallowed hard. "What was that you wanted to show me on your phone?"

"Oh, right." She scrolled her finger across the screen. "Gus from the gas station has been busy gossiping. You're gonna wanna be careful." She passed over the device.

Annamae took it with a trembling hand and scanned the snippet posted on—of all things—the gas station attendant's social media page. His status update included a grainy security photo that could have been anyone, especially since she was wearing glasses and a scarf. But judging by the number of Likes and Shares, all of Beulah had already seen the news online. How long before the Atlanta media got wind of this?

Annamae passed over the phone. "Thank you. I appreciate the heads up." Would her grandmother help her hide out until she could figure out a way to plant herself in the carriage house and recoup? She could only hope. "I'd like to surprise Hazel Mae now, if I may. She's—ah—an old friend."

"Hazel has always had the most interesting friends." The

CATHERINE MANN & JOANNE ROCK

woman laughed as if this was a great joke, but she made the call for Hazel to come to the commons area, leaving Annamae free to explore more of the downstairs of the retirement home. A game room played host to three ladies bickering over a jigsaw puzzle and two men snoozing between moves on a chessboard. At least, she hoped they were snoozing.

Past the game room a muffled hint of music and counting suggested dance lessons or a workout of some sort. The scent of chlorine—evident even under the stronger odors of furniture polish and Old Spice—made her think a swimming pool or spa tub lurked behind one of the doors off the main corridor. Finally, she found an empty room with a few shelves of books and settled in to wait. But Bobbi, the desk attendant, was right on her heels.

"Hazel will be right down, Ms. Jessup." Bobbi straightened a few of the books on the built-in shelves. "She's going to be so excited to see you. She and her friend, Ruby, love *Acting Up.*"

"Really?" Surprised, Annamae knew the over-sixty demographic wasn't the one that producers targeted with the show. Did Hazel watch to keep tabs on her granddaughter? Or was the older woman even aware of their connection? After Delilah's lies about the Smith family, Annamae couldn't be sure how much they knew about her.

"They were all up in arms when your youngest sister cheated on her psychology final exam last year." The woman leaned into the doorjamb, launching into a diatribe about favorite scenes from Annamae's last season.

"She didn't really cheat." One of many ways the editing process worked to the director's advantage.

But the desk attendant didn't hear her while she chattered about how upset her fiancé and parents must be over the broken engagement. She never mentioned anything about Hazel having a family connection to anyone on the show, so Annamae felt certain either Hazel was unaware or purposely hadn't shared the information.

Interesting either way.

"Bobbi, did you call for me?" An older woman appeared in the hallway outside the door. Head wrapped in a white towel like a turban, she wore a yellow and purple caftan covering her whole body from slender shoulders to dainty feet in flip-flops with daisies between the toes.

The woman looked as if she'd been in the middle of a sauna or a massage, her face scrubbed clean of makeup, every wrinkle exposed. Still, her skin was lovely, all things considered. The crow's feet around her eyes only made the vivid blue of her irises more striking. The laugh lines around her mouth settled into comfortable places as she smiled, and for a moment she didn't look any older than Annamae's mother.

"Hi, Ms. Smith." Annamae stepped forward, suddenly nervous. As she walked closer she realized her grandmother was taller than her. "I'm Annamae and I'm—"

"I know exactly who you are, darlin'." The older woman's smile widened as she reached past Bobbi to stroke her granddaughter's cheek.

Annamae's eyes went misty and despite the mess of her over-processed hair, the guilt of her break up and the refusal of Heath Lambert to be her landlord, she was so glad she'd come to Beulah. She couldn't believe she'd been deprived of her grandmother her whole life.

Leaning back, Hazel Mae clasped her hands to her chest for an emotionally charged moment before glancing over her shoulder.

Once Bobbi had disappeared and the hallway was empty, the older woman stepped deeper into the room, dragging Annamae with her. She clutched Annamae's arm with two hands, her eyes narrowing.

"What in Sam Hill are you doing here?"

Chapter Three

ANNAMAE STUMBLED BACK against a coffee table at her grandmother's harsh tone. Not that she should be surprised... hadn't Delilah insisted the alligator hunter's mother was mean as a snake? But right up to this second she hadn't realized how much she'd been hoping her mother had lied about that, as she'd hidden so many things about Annamae's father and his family.

"I don't understand—" she began, uncertain and regretting ever coming to Beulah. "I thought—"

"How kind of you to want to volunteer!" Hazel Mae exclaimed loudly, turning her head as if to project her voice as far as possible. "That sounds wonderful." Then, lowering her voice to a whisper again, she ducked closer. "The walls have ears here, even though they all need hearing aids."

"Um..." Annamae had no idea what to make of this woman. Was Hazel Mae delusional? Suffering early dementia?

"No one knows we're related," Hazel Mae insisted. "I suggest we keep it that way and if I were you, young lady, I would maintain a low profile. That means staying away from the gas station, the diner, and the retirement home." She ticked them off on manicured fingers. "And that dye job isn't fooling anyone. I'd go dark brunette. Dye the brows too." Her eyes tracked over Annamae's features. "Although I like the blonde."

"Thank you. That is, I appreciate the suggestions, but I came here hoping to ask you some questions about..." She bit her lip. "My father. My biological dad."

Hazel Mae's eyes went wide. She turned to look over her shoulder again, then glared at Annamae.

"Honey, *you* might not mind having your life story plastered all over the Internet, but I have skeletons that are very comfortable in their closets, thank you very much." She grabbed a paper off the coffee table behind Annamae and jammed it in her hand. "That's a flyer for the retirement home's community garden project. It's a total flop and no one ever shows up to hoe tomatoes but me. Meet me near the marigold bed by the fountain tomorrow morning and we'll talk there."

Before Annamae could argue, Hazel had an arm around her shoulders, steering her toward the door and down the hallway past Bobbi's desk.

"You are an angel to consider volunteering your time to bring attention to the aging veteran community. I think the local VA hospital is the best place to start, but I'm so glad we got to visit." Hazel must have done theater at some point, or else she was used to dialing up her volume for hard-of-hearing friends because her voice boomed loud enough for the whole first floor to hear.

"Of course." Annamae smiled, too well-schooled in peacekeeping to defy her grandmother and insist on answers to her questions.

Besides, if the meeting in the marigolds panned out, she could quiz her then.

"Thank you, darlin'. And good luck to you!" Hazel opened the front door with one hand and gently shoved Annamae toward the threshold where Bagel was already barking.

Thanking the dog sitter, she made tracks toward her VW Bug. She couldn't wait until tomorrow. But first, she would find her way back through those apple orchard fortress gates one way or another.

WYNN NEEDED BETTER technology if he wanted to survive three more weeks in Beulah, especially if he was going to let Annamae Jessup back on the property. He'd wrestled with the idea ever since he'd let her leave the first time, but he kept coming back to the fear that he'd put her in danger. He had no idea how close his enemies were. He'd like to think no one had a clue where he'd disappeared after he left Miami, but he was positive that the Dimitri family would have allocated considerable resources to find him.

He wouldn't let an innocent get caught in that crossfire again.

If he acted fast, he might be able to get her settled into the carriage house by nightfall. But only if she promised to lay low for a few weeks.

Otherwise... he didn't want to think about the otherwise. He did not want to get witness protection services involved in the three-ring circus of securing a television personality.

Now Wynn walked the perimeter of the eight-foot fence that some paranoid farmer had once used to encompass his prize apple trees and wondered how long he could count on the electric wiring to keep out unwanted company.

The beeper on his hip chimed while he secured a loose nail on a post along the back of the property. There'd been a gate on this side of the fence at one point, but Wynn had welded it shut before moving onto the grounds. Trip wires and alarms were set.

The place was secure.

"Lambert." He wedged the intercom receiver between his shoulder and his ear so he could keep working. He liked farm life just fine, but his crop wasn't nearly as important as security.

"It's Annamae Jessup, Mr. Lambert. I thought I'd follow up with you about the carriage house. Do you have a few minutes?"

"Actually, I was just about to contact you." Tucking the

bent nail in his pocket, he decided the rest of the fence repair would have to wait until tomorrow. No sense lingering around the fence if Annamae and her entourage lurked nearby.

"You were?" Her happiness transcended the piss-poor sound quality of the old-fashioned speaker system. He'd been so focused on better surveillance, he hadn't bothered with the sound.

While the woman was on her mysterious errand, he'd researched her online enough to familiarize himself with her storyline on the reality TV show—knew that she played the part of the good daughter in a household full of attention-seeking females. But he would be wise to remember that was just a role she'd been assigned. He wasn't about to get sucked in by a fake demeanor.

"If you're serious about wanting privacy while you're in town—."

"One hundred percent." She cut him off, her words blaring overtop of his since they both couldn't talk at the same time on this speaker system. "And if you wouldn't mind opening the back gate soon, I would really, really appreciate it. I'm pretty sure someone was following me earlier."

Wynn's feet stalled beneath him like a dead tractor. He shoved a hammer into the tool belt at his waist.

"Following you?" The back of his neck itched in warning. "A celebrity watcher, some kind of autograph seeker?" He hoped. "Or the media maybe?"

"That's the funny thing." She cleared her throat and in the background he could hear her dog panting—almost as if he had his muzzle right up to the microphone. "I didn't see any flashes or lenses, which is kind of weird for the people who normally stalk me. I thought it was someone who worked on your farm since he seemed more preoccupied with the grounds than with me."

What the hell was she talking about? He ground his teeth.

"Listen carefully to me." He gripped the beeper intercom harder, his thumb pressing the Plexiglas until it blurred the readout. "Is there anyone with you now?"

"No. A minor miracle since—"

"I'm opening the gate. Drive through fast." Tension clamped his head and stiffened his joints while he wondered who she'd seen. Probably just a curious local, but—Damn.

Without waiting for her response, he pressed the button on the remote opener and forced himself to wait a three-count before he closed it again. He might not care for this woman's upper crust air of entitlement or her self-involved manners, but he wouldn't allow an innocent to get caught up in the mess his life had become. A woman in the public eye couldn't make a better target for the people Wynn was hiding from and he needed to do everything in his power to make sure she remained out of their sight.

Once he had her settled, he'd figure out who was following her.

ANNAMAE HAD WON.

She was so used to being the overlooked sister that she almost couldn't believe that for once in her life she was calling her own shots. But she'd left Atlanta. Gotten a pet. Met her grandmother. And now she'd convinced Beulah, Alabama's sexiest hermit to rent her his carriage house, effectively winning their standoff.

It had been a banner day, but she'd been determined not to give up until she got what she wanted. And she wanted – needed – the solitude of that carriage house to get over losing her fiancé, wrecking her life and disappointing her family. She also needed the solitude to bolster herself for the inevitable showdown when her parents decided to confront her.

Old VW jostling along every pothole, Annamae steered down the long driveway toward Heath's house shortly before sunset, pleasantly surprised she'd convinced him to let her stay. Either way, she wouldn't turn her nose up at a break.

After the strange visit with her grandmother, Annamae needed to regroup and plan for their meeting tomorrow. The beginning stages of senility might account for some of Hazel Mae's odd behavior, but what if she truly had information to share about Annamae's father?

Besides, getting to know her grandmother would be easier if Annamae lived a stone's throw from the retirement center that Hazel Mae had warned her not to visit. She hoped the marigold patch was as quiet as the older woman believed. Annamae had the feeling her soon-to-be landlord would not appreciate any more celebrity buzz coming too close to his private apple haven.

He was definitely not the sort of guy who lobbied to meet her and her sisters just to be on television. Even though show producers would have fainted to have such a—er— *virile* man making appearances on the show. They'd asked for months to get Boone on *Acting Up* last season, but his game schedule had been too busy. And Heath Lambert was every bit as good-looking, along with a dangerous, tough guy edge.

Speaking of Heath…

Holy shitake mushrooms, he was hotter than she remembered. Damn it. Her memory of their last meeting had been defined by his efforts to judge her, to pigeonhole her as a brainless TV personality and a liar. She'd come away with a vague impression of hard, unforgiving eyes and rough, angular features.

Apparently her brain had edited out the memories of broad, tanned hands and muscular arms. And she'd been denied the view of six-pack abs last time, a sight she saw for all of two seconds as he pulled a shirt over his head on his way toward her car.

"No one was at the gate when you pulled in, right?" He covered the ground between them in long, purposeful strides, his focus narrowing to just her in a way she found disconcerting.

"Right. Just me and my dog." She didn't bother rolling up the window since the top was down anyway. She left her keys in the ignition and unfolded out of the driver's seat while Bagel ran a few circles around her feet until he spotted a cat to chase.

Or, as it happened, a cat to bark at.

The black and white tomcat perched on a forgotten old brick well merely glared down at Bagel with a haughty feline stare.

Annamae smoothed a hand over her scarf, tucking a stray lock of brittle, over processed hair back under the silk, and then regretted it as Heath's eyes followed the movement. Instinct told her this guy expected flirtation and feminine wiles from her and those same instincts said he didn't respect those kinds of games.

Too bad her need to smooth the wrinkles from the skirt of her dress didn't have anything to do with a desire to flirt and everything to do with feeling rumpled, tired and out of sorts. She wished she could turn off the internal voices that second-guessed what everyone around her was thinking, a habit engrained growing up in a household that had been watched constantly. But like it or not, she cared what other people thought of her.

"Did you notice anything in particular about the car following you, or the person driving the vehicle?" Dark concern transformed his eyes and his whole face as the sun dropped lower in the sky behind him, casting purple light around them.

Feminine awareness fluttered even though she told it to damn well shut up. Now was not the time to take a sudden shine to bad boys. She had enough trouble on her heels.

"I'm always being followed. I stopped taking notes a long time ago." She would not capitalize on his worry for her since she'd weathered plenty of unwanted attention in Atlanta. "It comes with the territory when you're on TV. I just didn't want to upset the people at the retirement community with a lot of cameras. Besides, it was your guy this time, right?"

Was she missing something here?

His expression went even more ominous.

"Why would you think that?" His jaw flexed forbiddingly, as if she'd somehow lied or cheated or otherwise deceived him.

"Because I saw him just outside the back fence earlier," she clarified, hoping she wasn't getting his farm help in too much trouble. "It was the same person you had trimming trees along the fence when I arrived earlier today to see the carriage house."

He reached into her car, pulled out her keys and passed them over.

From anyone else, that gesture might have seemed presumptuous. But Annamae had the feeling he would have done the same thing for anyone. Heath wasn't a man to open a woman's door, but he made sure nothing dangerous lurked on the other side.

"I don't employ anyone but me." He gestured toward the house. "Would you mind describing this person to me in more detail? I don't like the idea of someone making themselves at home around here without my knowledge."

She followed him without thinking, without weighing her options. Wasn't it that kind of reflexive attitude in life that got her on a television show she hadn't wanted to be a part of in the first place?

Forcing herself to stop, she waited for him to notice. To turn and face her. Bagel sat beside her, waiting with her.

"Aren't we going to talk about the carriage house rental?" That's the reason she was here. Not to do him a favor by pointing the finger at some unsuspecting farm hand, who probably only wanted a job.

"I can't think about the rental until I get this taken care of, Ms. Jessup. I'm sure you'll understand."

"It's Annamae. Not Ms. Jessup. And I *don't* understand. I've had the worst day of my life, and I think I'm going to lose my mind if I can't close my eyes and try to put it behind me soon." She'd been so pleased to get through his all-mighty gates, but maybe he'd only wanted the scoop on her vagrant fan.

But damn it, her life was in an absolute shambles. Tomorrow was supposed to be her wedding day. The happiest day of her life. If all had gone according to plan, she would have been dancing under the stars with Boone in twenty-four hours, soon to start a fairytale life – with a man she didn't love according to a British radio talk show host.

God, she needed a bed and bucket of ice cream. She forced herself to listen to Heath, her eyes locking on his dark brown gaze.

"I've got enemies, Annamae, and it occurs to me that you could be in some trouble if you don't come clean about who you saw skulking around the property earlier today. Do you understand?"

What had he said? Her brain was a scramble.

They'd gotten closer somehow while he was speaking. Close enough that she could feel the warmth radiating off him right through his t-shirt. She had an absurd amount of awareness for this man, noticing all sorts of things she shouldn't.

Chemistry, some knowing part of her brain informed her.

It had been a piece that had been missing for her with Boone, as much as she hadn't wanted to face it. Impossibly, she was even more reluctant to face the truth that she *did* feel it for this surly, bossy, reclusive stranger. What was wrong with her?

"What kind of enemies?" she found herself asking, grateful her brain had seized on some topic that didn't involve attraction. Awareness. Pheromones.

Her mouth had gone dry in the last minute, however. She knew because she had to lick her lips to get even those few words out.

"You know how you have some secrets you don't want to share, Red?" His voice rumbled between them, making her realize they were still too close.

Her hand went to her scarf, but she didn't want to take the thing off. The hair underneath was far worse than having him call her Red.

"Don't we all?" She turned her attention toward the carriage house before she leaned closer to him.

She didn't even think she *liked* Heath, so it bothered her that she felt this... alive, electric intensity around him.

"Exactly. We all have secrets. You keep yours. I'll keep mine. But the only reason I'm letting you stay here is because you said you wanted to keep a low profile. If that's not still the case, I'd suggest you keep driving. There's a bigger town south of Beulah where it will be easier to find a place—."

"I'm staying." She dug in her purse to find her wallet again.

"Then come to the house and I'll find you some clean sheets and towels." He turned on his heel and headed in the direction of the big house. His house.

Bagel took off after him, yipping happily.

It was a nice offer. A thoughtful gesture, even, since she didn't have much of anything with her besides a few bargain store dresses. But she couldn't deny that his offer to share sheets with her had led her thoughts in an interesting direction for a few breathless seconds.

She was making a lie of her "good girl" role more with each passing second.

Hurrying to catch up with his long strides, she wondered if it was foolish of her not to quiz him more about the nature of his "enemies." He didn't seem like a paranoid farmer stockpiling weapons for a zombie apocalypse, but then again, who knew? Maybe she'd been too distracted by the way his low-slung jeans hugged his lean hips to ask the right questions.

Tonight, she was too weary from this day to even care. She hadn't known how much stress the last few years had piled on her shoulders until she'd crossed the Georgia State line.

Now, Heath held the screen door open for her while two cats and Bagel darted in ahead of her.

She stepped into a large farmhouse kitchen with old wooden cabinets and a big white sink under a faucet that looked like an old well spout. The appliances were all new though. The outside of the Lambert farm might look run down, but someone had put money into upgrading the kitchen. Wrought iron pendant lamps hung over an island where a handful of old farming books sat open to diagrams of trees and how to graft branches.

Heath closed the volumes when he saw her looking at them.

"Can I get you something to eat?"

"No thank you." She was starving, actually, but she

didn't want to spend any more time here with him than she needed to.

Her emotions were all over the place and the rogue attraction was seriously unwelcome. Maybe she just needed a good night's rest to put this day—and memories of Heath's abs—well behind her.

"I'll box up a few staples for you to take to the carriage house." He pulled open the door to a huge walk-in pantry and gestured toward the island. "Have a seat while you wait and we'll talk."

She hoped cookies and ice cream were staples for him, even though his physique suggested otherwise.

"This is very nice of you," she called to him while he shuffled things around in the pantry. "I'm so grateful to you for letting me stay."

"I said we need to talk. There will be ground rules."

His terse words shouldn't have surprised her.

"It's funny you say that." She turned a stainless steel toaster toward her to check her hair in the reflective surface. Straightening her scarf, she cursed herself for not taking more time to scrub out the developing solution from her hair in the sink when she'd left the salon that morning. "I'm always telling my parents they need to set more ground rules for the girls."

Her sisters were growing up too wild, continually rewarded for pushing boundaries that boosted ratings. Annamae had been livid when the youngest—a high school junior—brought over a twenty-year-old guy for a family meal. All the more so because their mother fawned all over him.

It was gross.

"I mean privacy ground rules," he clarified. "If you're serious about laying low, there's no social media. No cell phone that someone could track, not unless you're willing to go back into town and invest in seriously high scramblers. And no use of credit cards."

"Right. I know." She'd thought through all that on the drive to Beulah. "I picked up some extra disposable phones in case I need to make calls."

The same kind she spotted on his kitchen table, in fact. In a three-pack.

"Have you used a check or credit card in Alabama?" He hauled out a box overflowing with bags of pasta, paper products and something that looked like protein bars.

No cookies yet. The chances decreased that his freezer sported ice cream.

"No. I paid cash for my gas. And my cell phone has been off. I called you with one of the pay-by-the-minute phones I bought just outside of Atlanta."

"Good. That's good." He assembled another box from a stack of cardboard stored alongside the refrigerator.

His distracted approval made her feel ridiculously proud of herself. She thumbed through the book on the counter—a farmer's almanac. Someone had made little drawings in the margins with diagrams of a garden.

"I am very content to dig in here for a few weeks and let the world forget all about me." She turned to a recipe section and remembered she couldn't lock herself into Heath's carriage house forever. "Although I did promise my grandmother I'd meet her in the retirement home's garden tomorrow."

"Your grandmother." He scowled. "Isn't this the first place folks will look for you to run? To your family?"

"Don't worry, no one outside of the immediate family knows we're related, and as far as they're concerned we're estranged. I wasn't even sure she would want to see me. But she actually got all strangely protective of me,"—at least, that's what Annamae hoped had been her motive—"and told me to meet her in the garden tomorrow morning when no one would be around."

"So she's trying to help you keep the low profile?" Heath went to the fridge and pulled out eggs, milk and butter, tossing them all in the box.

"I guess. I'd never met her before today." Annamae shrugged. "Got any wine to spare? Or coffee?"

He produced both so quickly, shoving both in the box, that she was tempted to ask for the best, fastest place to get ice cream, but she wasn't supposed to leave. She could always bake cookies.... But she hated to reveal all her food vices at once. *Acting Up* had almost given her an eating disorder during the first season.

"Your bio online doesn't say anything about a connection to this town at all. Or a grandmother who lives here, even an estranged one. So maybe you're right that no one will look for you here." Heath moved to a drawer stocked with utensils and found some spoons, measuring cups and a corkscrew.

"You ran a background check anyhow?" She enjoyed watching him move around his kitchen, cats lazing at his feet as if they hung out there all the time.

She found a pen and made a few notes while he worked.

"Told you I would." He stuffed some paper plates in the box and one coffee mug. "So, what's the deal with your grandmother?"

"She's my biological father's mother. But I've never met my real father either. And my stepfather's wealth does a great job of hiding things he wants kept hidden, so there's no mention of my dad anywhere online."

Heath nodded as he stalked over to the fridge and pulled out two longnecks.

"Beer?" he offered.

"I'd better not. I'm going to wait to have that glass of wine until I get settled in the new space." She did not need her inhibitions lowered in front of him when she was an emotional wreck and feeling mighty vulnerable. "I wrote down a description of that guy I saw trimming the hedges." She passed him a napkin with details written on it. "If you don't mind, I'd like to settle into the carriage house before it gets any darker."

Twilight was going to turn to full dark soon, the sky outside pale purple. She needed to leave her rent and go to bed.

"I can turn the fuse box from here. You'll have power and—in another hour or two—some hot water." He was already reading over her notes.

"Thank you." She nodded as she slid one of the boxes he'd packed closer to her. She could see a new set of sheets still in the package at the bottom of one of them.

"What time are you seeing your grandmother?" he asked, pulling a long swallow from the beer bottle, giving her too much time to watch the movement of his throat. To see the wet shine of his lower lip.

"Nine." She was ridiculously thirsty all of a sudden.

"I'll meet you to walk you out a side entrance through the orchard. I don't like the idea of people watching the roads in and out of this place."

"Okay, I appreciate the offer." She hugged a box to her chest and backed toward the door. Bagel hurried to beat her there, doggy nails clicking against the floor.

"I could help you settle in." He scooped up the other box and followed her toward the door.

Then reached over her head to prop open the screen for her.

The scent of male sweat and faded aftershave should not have smelled so damn good. Temptingly so on a day when it would be worse than horrible to act on that temptation.

"I'll be fine on my own." She needed to be alone.

To repent for being a crappy fiancée. God, had she really been about to get married to the wrong man? And now she was drooling over a total stranger who didn't even keep good ice cream in his house?

"At least let me carry this to your car." He let the screen bang closed behind them as they walked out into the growing dimness.

"Thanks again for all your help." She hastened her step and stuffed her box in the backseat of the open convertible. "I left cash for the rent under the toaster."

"Right. My main concern is no social media. No cell phone. No way of leading anyone here." His expression was hard. Shuttered.

He leaned down to put the second box beside the first while Bagel darted into the passenger seat through the open driver's side door.

"You won't regret letting me stay," she promised, then wondered if anyone would trust her word again after the way she'd ditched Boone today.

Her heart hurt as she slid into the driver's seat. Heath closed the door behind her, then leaned to rest his arms on the top of the door.

"Will he come after you?" he asked quietly. "The baseball player?"

Surprising her. How had he guessed she was thinking about her former fiancé?

"No."

"How can you be sure?"

"Trust me. I'm certain." That admission—and the way it forced her to acknowledge the truth underneath it—sank deeper than any other pain she'd felt today.

Heath nodded. Straightened.

"Then he didn't deserve you, Red." He reached to give her scarf a gentle tug, leaving it in place. "Sleep well."

He stalked off toward the main house while Annamae's scalp tingled, fingers of a phantom pleasure tripping down her spine.

And although the carriage house was a stone's throw up the road, she punched the gas to get there as fast as she could.

Chapter Four

EIGHTY-SEVEN MISSED CALLS.

Half of them from her mother. A few from Lindsey offering help and a place to stay if she needed it.

None of them from her ex-fiancé.

She'd checked the voicemail from another one of the disposable phones and then set it aside. She should feel horribly disappointed. Instead, she felt relieved all the way to her toenails with chipped polish. Clearly, she'd made the right decision in calling off the wedding. Had she made the right choice in running away though?

Too late for second guessing that. She was committed to this path for now. And right or wrong, she needed the breathing room. She needed answers.

Annamae wished she'd picked up more throwaway phones to check in so people wouldn't worry, but she couldn't afford to leave hers on and risk someone tracking her here. The media hadn't latched onto the sighting of her in Beulah, but just in case, she posted a message on social media about her trip out West to throw them off the scent, posting from a phone with no location tracking. Let them think she was on an extended road trip.

She needed privacy if she stood a chance of unearthing answers about her screwed-up choices. Answers she craved more than a bottomless bowl of butter pecan ice cream.

With a sigh, Annamae hefted the first box out of the Beetle, closing the red door with a swish of her hip.

She surveyed the carriage house silhouetted in the fading sun. In this softening light, the old building seemed inviting, the imperfections of a droopy shutter and faded paint looking artsy rather than run down. It didn't hold the glamor of her townhome of Atlanta, but the distressed wood and stone was homey, a good kind of worn-in. Like the Beetle. Simple. And God, she could use something simple as she sorted out her far too complicated life.

Annamae stepped around an overturned wheelbarrow with wildflowers sprouting out as she entered through the side entrance again. The wood door squeaked open and the house was awash in darkness. Bagel bounded inside, un-daunted by the lack of light, nails clicking against the wood floor, then quieting as he went airborne toward the fuzzy shape of what she hoped was a sofa. Balancing the box in one hand, she fumbled on the wall for the light switch.

The light flickered before stabilizing. Annamae pushed deeper into the living area, past the loveseat and coffee table and set her box down on the stretch of a sturdy bench that lined the back wall. The stately dark wood bench parked against stone walls made the carriage house seem like it had waltzed out of a fairytale. A few talking animals would complete the image.

"What do you think, Bagel?" Annamae cooed. The scruffy mutt wriggled his whole body but didn't utter a sound. Still, he was clearly adjusting well.

"Let's take a look around, buddy." She scooped him into her arms, his wiry fur tickly against her skin.

Room by room, Annamae flipped on lights, gauging her new space. She walked up the stairs to the loft bedroom. Sparse, but functional.

A full size bed was angled in one corner, and a single dresser with a mirror in the other. The wood floor squeaked as she circled the huge, open space. The bedroom sported a large, arched window that overlooked the majority of the apple orchard. The view would be beautiful at dawn. Part of her ached that she was here alone, so detached from everything she had ever known. No one to share the beauty with.

But a larger part of her was excited at the potential this place offered. There were no cameras, no faces she needed to wear.

She set Bagel down on the bed and he wiggled across the quilt over to the window. He stared outside, brown eyes alert.

"Are you going to be my tough guard dog?" Annamae laughed from the doorway. Bagel cocked his head to the side.

"We're going to be just fine here," she said.

Turning the light off, Annamae climbed back down the

rustic steps, Bagel close at her heels. She retrieved the final box from her car and made her way into the circa 1950s kitchen, complete with mint green cabinets and a black checkerboard tile floor.

She set the groceries on the red vinyl-topped table and started unloading. Peanut butter, a loaf of bread, crackers, and some cans of soup. No ice cream though. That would be one of her first purchases tomorrow once she was very sure the freezer worked well. She emptied the rest onto the table. A wrought iron chandelier of exposed lights bathed the room in a warm, yellow glow.

It would take some getting used to, all this...possibility. A new dog, a new town. A new life. One she was completely in control of. And, a new man, maybe. Annamae's cheeks heated. She had only just called off her wedding.

And yet, she couldn't deny the electric feeling of being in Heath's presence. It was like being outside before a Southern summer storm struck. The air crackled with anticipation. It was crazy and so unlike her normally practical self.

Bagel splayed out on the floor, his belly against the cool tile. The pup looked wiped. She huffed a chunk of over-processed hair off her brow and turned on a fan by the sink, then opened a window. Okay, tried to open a window. She pushed harder, harder still and then ... *whoosh*. The window slid upward and a gust of wind swept in carrying the scent of apple blossoms.

Sagging back against the counter, she allowed herself a

blessed moment to just breathe. How often did she stand still and simply – breathe without worrying about gasping for air? Well, other than in yoga class but that was filmed and broadcast so it didn't count.

She angled the fan toward her and started to put away the few groceries Heath had given her. She turned over her feelings in her mind, trying to get a read on her emotions. Heath was handsome, in the rough-around-the-edges sort of way. But she could count on one hand the number of boyfriends she'd had in her entire life. It wasn't in her nature to be attracted to a guy hours after breaking off an engagement.

As she put the cans of soup in the top cupboard, she forced herself to refocus on why she had driven to Beulah. To find out about the father she had never known, to discover a whole other side to herself. To get her life in order.

Heath certainly wasn't going to provide her with any of those answers. But her grandmother could. She needed to glean all she could from Hazel Mae, needed to figure out who she was when the cameras weren't rolling. There was no scripted role here. There was only the opportunity to find herself. And to do that, she needed her grandmother.

As she closed the cabinet and reached into her purse for a box of hair color, Annamae resolved to make tomorrow as productive as possible.

WYNN HOOKED AN arm around a branch and hefted himself up higher to survey the land in front of him. He was restless. He didn't like the idea of someone poking around his grounds. Not when he was so close to leaving this place. He'd submitted Annamae's description of the man hanging around outside the fence to a contact back in Miami, wanting to cover all bases in case he'd been found. The upcoming trial still weighed heavy on his mind. And the added publicity of Annamae didn't do anything to ease those worries. He hoped interest in her would die down and that they would both have well-deserved privacy.

He absently checked the blossoms on the branch around him. The white petals were perfect, fragrant and full. Maybe the crop wouldn't be all bad. He could only hope.

The creak of door hinges from the carriage house snapped him into focus. His eyes automatically trailed to the source of the sound, the source of his midnight dreams.

Annamae.

And not the Annamae from before, the glammed-up girl with a scarf trailing in the wind. She was dressed in worn-looking jeans, cowgirl boots, and an oversized t-shirt. Her hair was piled in a messy bun on top of her head. Her hair wasn't bleached blonde white any longer. Today, her cara-mel-colored hair caught the sun, a warm honey look that suited her more than the highlights he'd seen when he googled her online.

Strands had fallen out, framing her face, making her look softer. He could almost forget she was a celebrity. She looked casual, so down to earth, a far cry from the perfectly styled girl on television. The early morning sun glinted off of her sunglasses as she walked toward the orchard, more particularly, toward the very tree Wynn perched, watching her.

"Hey Red," he called out, lowering himself down a limb. "Sleep well?"

She craned her neck until she spotted him. "Were you waiting up there for me?"

"Waiting for you? I've been killing leaf hoppers for almost two hours." He chose a limb just over her head and took a seat, balancing his spray bottle to show her. Chasing bugs and beetles wasn't as dangerous as chasing criminals, but they were easier to squash. "I start my day early. I'm guessing you don't, diva girl?"

"Filming begins before sunup," she said with a defensive tone, sliding down to sit at the base of the tree. "Is that all natural pesticide?"

She squinted up at the plain white spray bottle he held.

"This concoction is my trade secret. I make it myself." He didn't like thinking they had anything in common— whether it was rising at dawn or an interest in organic farming. "I'll bet someone else does your hair and makeup, chooses your clothes. Brings you breakfast."

"A whole crew of people, actually." Her head thudding

back against the trunk, she eyed his work boots. "I've learned to nap in the stylist's chair and skip the food."

"Didn't your mom tell you breakfast is the most important meal of the day?"

Her jaw set. "My mother told me every meal of the day added pounds in addition to the ten added by the camera."

"That's too bad," he said, giving her a sidelong glance, "because you could certainly use at least ten or fifteen more."

She gazed back at him, shock evident on her face. Her brows arched. "Did you just insult me?"

"Only if you care what I think about the way you look." And he let himself look long and hard on the stretch of her legs, those legs he'd fantasized about until he'd given up sleep altogether.

Bagel sat beside her, sniffing in the grass.

She hitched a hand on her hip. "You're fishing for a reaction."

"Maybe," he said with a nonchalant shrug. He was fishing. She was intriguing for a runaway minor celebrity. Different than anyone else he'd met. And although their circumstances were worlds apart, they were both forced into isolation.

"Why would you want to push for a reaction from me? I thought you didn't even like me."

"That has nothing to do with lust," he said evenly.

Truthfully.

The air crackled so hot between them he could swear the

CATHERINE MANN & JOANNE ROCK

dew steamed right off the grass.

She shot to her feet, swiping her wrist across her mouth as she finished chewing. "Wow, uhm," she muttered, dusting the dirt off her bottom, "this conversation got uncomfortable fast. In case you don't remember, I was engaged yesterday."

"And today," he said, closing his hand around the trunk as he resisted the urge to dust in the exact same space, "you're not. You don't appear heartbroken to me."

Annamae's cheeks burned. Good, he thought. So she could be riled.

She scooped her purse off the ground. "I need to see my grandmother."

The sun tucked behind a cloud. "Be careful out there, Red. I hear too many stories of people getting into wrecks racing away from their fans."

"I always drive safely, even when I'm being followed." She hitched her bag over her shoulder and glanced back at him. "I've learned to go safely to the nearest police station."

He watched the sway of her hips as she strode toward her car and he mumbled, "Good plan."

And one that would only work until the day a car pulled in front of her, beside her, and tailgated her. He had seen it happen in chases when he was on the force. Miami had its own share of celebrity mishaps.

She was too innocent, damn it, and he couldn't let her go out there alone.

Decision made, Wynn swung down out of the tree and

landed surefooted on the ground. She might be good at watching for people who tailed her.

But she'd never been followed by *him*.

ANNAMAE LOCKED HER red Beetle and glanced around the area. The parking lot was still, undisturbed. There was no movement, except for a dull breeze that set the grass dancing. No one had followed her. She loosed a sigh of relief as she jogged along the sidewalk toward the path to the garden. She was running late after her talk with Heath. She could still feel the heat of his eyes as he'd watched her.

Wanted her.

A want she couldn't help feeling in return.

Just a healthy, normal attraction. Right?

A really strong attraction.

Adjusting her sunglasses, Annamae stepped lightly on the slate path that wound into the marigold garden. Pockets of morning glories and rose bushes welcomed her into the thick of the garden. The red of the roses caught her eye and for a moment, her mind turned away from the task of talking to her grandmother.

For the briefest moment, her mind wandered back again to this morning and her exchange with Heath. Did she care what he thought of her? Should she care? He was rough-spun, so blunt and honest. He clearly wasn't interested in empty flattery or fifteen minutes on screen with her. He had nothing to gain from their interaction.

Focus, she reprimanded herself, scanning the neat fields of the community garden just outside the hedgerow around the walking paths through the flowers. She searched for a trace of her grandmother. Annnnnd nothing. No sign of her.

Marigolds encircled the marble fountain, a trio of angels spewing water from their mouths. The path curved around the right side of the orange flowers and cherub trio. Tall stalks of sunflowers hugged the other side of the path.

The back edge of the garden was lined with a cluster of Slash Pines standing like guardians of this little sanctuary, benches strategically placed for elderly residents to take a breather whenever needed. The white flowers of witch alder swayed beneath the pines, making the garden feel full of life.

But absent of her grandmother, Annamae noted. Her stomach plummeted.

Was Hazel Mae the sort of woman to stand her up? She had been absent in her life for all this time. This whole impulsive plan—

Out of the corner of her eye, Annamae noticed there was a floppy sun hat in the midst of the witch alder, a hat filled with little white flowers. It had to be her grandmother.

Was everyone in her life going to make a habit of hanging in trees and shrubbery to talk to her?

"Are you sure no one followed you?" Hazel Mae asked in a stage whisper, eyebrows arched as Annamae drew close.

It was a question Annamae was already growing used to hearing.

"I'm certain." She had a sneaking suspicion she would become an expert at hiding in plain sight over the next few months after the way she broke off her engagement.

"Your disguise is good. You always did like to play dress up as a little one," she said, stepping out from the bushes. Hazel Mae swooped her hands along her t-shirt, brushing off stray twigs from the faded carnival logo.

Shock washed through Annamae faster than the water from the angels' mouths. "How do you know that?"

"Your mother let me see you some, in the early days before she found her a new husband." She pressed on the knees of her jeans as she sat slowly on a bench. "I have pictures. I keep them in an album in my room."

"You do? I thought ..." Her voice trailed off. Her mother had intentionally misled her. For years, Annamae had been allowed to believe that her grandmother was ashamed of her, that she had never wanted to meet her. That she even blamed Annamae for the way her son had left for Australia.

"What?" Her grandmother watched her with a sharp intensity.

"I thought that we never met."

Her lips pressed tight, thinning. "That I just walked away from you?"

"Didn't you?" The accusation came out sharper than Annamae intended. She couldn't help it. Years of frustration pressed against her tongue.

"In the end, I didn't have much choice." Bitterness edged into Hazel Mae's words. What had Annamae's mother said to keep her away?

And why would it matter now?

"I'm an adult now. There's this thing called the telephone. Or the Internet. Or the good old U.S. Postal Service."

"True enough." She folded her arms over her chest. "Is that why you came here to Beulah? To chew me out for being a crummy grammy?"

Annamae shook her head and let out a wavering sigh as she sat beside her grandmother. "I'm not doing this right. I haven't done much right lately."

"You walked out before you married the wrong man." Hazel patted her granddaughter's knee. "I'd say that means you did something right."

Something right? This was the last place she'd expected to get absolution, from someone who barely knew her. But she couldn't resist asking, "How do you know he and I were wrong for each other?"

Her grandmother leaned in, conspirator-like, the scent of gardenia perfume and those flowers in her hat mixing. "I hate to break it to you, sweetheart, but you're not that good of an actress. You weren't really in love with Boone any more than he was in love with you."

Ouch. That hurt.

But not as much as it should, which spoke volumes. She'd already half guessed as much anyway. "Then would you like to explain why we almost got married – since you seem to have all the answers? Because, quite frankly, I'm coming up dry here."

Hazel Mae smiled at her as she snapped a bloom from a bush and tucked it in her granddaughter's gathered-up hair. "You're a people pleaser." She tucked in another tiny blossom on the other side. "You wanted everyone to love you, so you went along with the plan to marry the golden boy of Atlanta."

"You're making me sound like a wimp."

"A wimp wouldn't be here confronting me." She tucked another blossom in her hair before cradling her cheek briefly in a lotion soft hand.

Tears burned along with a pressing question she couldn't fathom.

"You say I was going along with the plan. But what about Boone? If Boone didn't love me, then why did he propose?" What had been visible on camera that had been hidden from her? She desperately wanted answers about her failed attempt at happily-ever-after. Even if they hurt. She needed to know.

"My guess? He thought it was time to take that next step in his life and you are a pretty girl. He was probably infatuated. Maybe even a little smitten, but being with you was safe. Plenty of men flinch at deeper emotions."

Seriously? That was it? She was convenient? They'd both been part of one big reality show hoax because real life was too scary? That meant she and Boone both were big fat cowards after all. Although she couldn't help but wonder how many people fell into that same trap off-camera.

"Is that what happened with my mom and dad?"

Snorting on a laugh, Hazel shook her head. "Oh not at all. They were deeply, passionately in love. The kind that heats up a room when they so much as walk through the door." She fanned herself with both hands. "That kind of love either lasts a lifetime or combusts. Your parents, well, they combusted. But at least they made you, so something very wonderful came of their love."

"He loved my mother so much he left for Australia?" That didn't seem to add up.

Hazel Mae's laughter faded along with her smile, sadness settling into her eyes. "He wasn't a steady kind of guy. He was the sort that had restless feet like his daddy."

"So when he heard my mother was pregnant with me, he left the country." That sounded like a step beyond restless feet to her.

"Actually, he asked her to go with him. He was going to strap you into a backpack for a walkabout."

She tried to envision her mother in outback gear trekking with wallabies and the image didn't come close to gelling. "My mom said no."

"She did."

"Figures."

"Hold on now. Life isn't always that simple. She said she didn't believe he would stick around for the long haul once they got there, and honestly, girlie, I'm not sure I can blame her. It's one thing to be a single mom in her own hometown. But to be in another country, left alone with no support system, that would be devastating."

The thought of her mother alone in a strange country with a baby was beyond scary. For any new parent. "My mom opted for security for my sake," she said, realizing it for the first time and more than a little stunned.

"She did."

"And so did I. Almost." Maybe she had inherited restless feet too. Maybe that's why security and constant invasive cameras were too high a cost for Annamae.

"Almost being the operative word." Her grandmother cocked her head to the side. "Instead, you came here for answers."

"I did, didn't I?"

Hazel Mae stared thoughtfully at her. Gently she said, "Did you find them?"

"Some, not all."

She still ached to know more about her father who'd abandoned her, but also didn't want to know him, the walkabout guy who ditched her—and ditched her mom, too. Feeling sorry for her mother was a new emotion, which brought up a whole new batch of questions. And the biggest question of all. "Gramma," the name unearthed from somewhere deep, maybe from buried memories of long ago play dates, "what do I do now?"

"Oh sweetheart, that's the easiest question of all. You do what any girl does after a bad breakup." She leaned forward. "You find a smoking hot man and have a fling."

Chapter Five

THE WHOLE DRIVE back to Heath's place, Annamae couldn't stop thinking about what her grandmother said about having an affair.

She steered her VW through the security gate in back, which somehow the press had not yet discovered. Could she really indulge in an affair?

Her grandmother's words rolled around in her mind. All of them. The parts about her parents, her father wanting to be a part of her life, but her mother being responsible and careful. So many shades of gray to something that had seemed black and white before.

No wonder she didn't have a clue about how to build a healthy relationship with so many mixed messages and misinformation. What a mess she would have made of her life if she'd actually gone through with marrying Boone. And what a time to realize they hadn't even slept together in over a month. How had *that* happened? They were supposed to be in love. Ready to get married. And yet they'd both been too busy—him with spring training, her with the show—for even a heavy petting make-out.

She didn't know if she was ready for an affair. But she did know she couldn't so much as consider the possibility until she had complete closure with Boone. And that meant talking to him.

She pulled up outside the carriage house and shifted the car into neutral, the air conditioner still blasting over her. She pulled out one of her throwaway phones and texted.

Please pick up your phone. We need to talk. She paused, knowing a simple plea wasn't enough. *If you don't call me back at,* she looked up the digits to the temporary phone and typed them in. Then finished her text with, *I will go to the press and tell them about the tattoo on your butt.*

Fifteen seconds later, her second throwaway phone rang.

"Annamae, damn it," Boone barked through the airwaves, "I made it clear I don't want to talk to you. Not now. Maybe not ever."

"Boone, I'm really sorry." Her voice was calm, despite her slamming chest.

"For dumping me? Or breaking my heart? Doing that on the radio and television, simultaneously?"

Guilt hammered her again. "All of the above. For any embarrassment I caused you. For not being brave enough to face you." For still not being brave enough to face the music in Atlanta. "For not figuring this out earlier. And most especially for any harm I did to your heart."

She threw in that last part just in case her grandmother was wrong, just in case maybe she had truly hurt this very perfect man.

"Harm to my heart?" He laughed darkly. "That sounds like some melodramatic line from your TV show."

Except it wasn't a line. She really wanted, needed, to know. "Did you love me?"

"That's a strange question to ask. We were a day away from being married." Yet he hadn't answered her question.

She rested her forehead on the steering wheel. "I know. And I'm asking."

"Annamae, are you asking to get back together again, because that's not going to happen. Ever."

"I realize that. Breaking up was the right thing to do. I just went about it the wrong way."

He went silent for a few heartbeats. "So what do you want?"

"I want us to be okay about this."

"To be friends?" He snorted. "Not likely."

"I should have handled things differently," she said again softly, regret making her ache all over.

"Yes, Annamae, you should have." Clearly, he wasn't cutting her any slack. And she didn't deserve it. "But it's done and we're over. So whatever absolution you wanted, consider it granted, move on, and Annamae? Don't call me again."

And just like that, the supposed love of her life hung up the phone on her.

It was over. Truly over. Well, other than the press gathered outside the front gate ready to tear her to pieces for dumping the Golden Boy of Atlanta.

She sagged back in her seat and stared at the rundown farm house with the hot landlord. A major part of her ached to act on the totally inappropriate, ill-timed hunger to hop into bed with him. To lose herself in mind blowing sex and forget what a mess her life was.

But right now, with her head such a jumble, adding one impulsive move on top of an already crazy impulsive breakup just didn't seem the wise thing to do. So she shut off the car and retreated to her carriage house where she intended to spend the rest of the weekend with a book and her dog while she figured out what the hell to do next.

TWO DAYS LATER, Wynn had to wonder what the hell was Annamae doing picking through his yard, triggering every alarm in his security system? And looking damn fine doing it in jeans that hugged every curve.

More distracting than the alarms chiming through his house.

He turned his back on the kitchen window and walked to the control panel in the mudroom. He punched in the code. Silence blanketed the house. He tipped his head from side to side, working the crick out of his neck that had a certain female's name written all over the knotted muscles even though she'd kept her word about a low profile the last few days. Tiger launched off a shelf lined with cleaning supplies, half of which were actually disguised stashes for weapons and cash for emergencies.

Palming the wall over the security system, he tapped the screen codes and cycled through the cameras that gave him a view of property, just to be certain. He had her to think about as well as himself now. Chances were his location was still secret, but thanks to that stupid picture Gus posted, the world knew she'd been sighted here. If the Dimitri mob found out his location, that would put her at risk.

Like it or not, she was tied to him now and the Dimitris would use anything at their disposal to shut down his testimony. He had an obligation to make sure she stayed safe and out of the public eye. This morning, he'd already called in a favor from some police force friends to keep an extra eye on the Dimitri family and their known henchmen—none of whom matched the description of the guy Annamae had seen lurking around the fence. He'd also ramped up his own security.

Although that was an iffy thing on a farm when small critters – and scruffy dogs – could set off an alarm.

He double-checked the different camera surveillance angles until he was confident no one else was on the property, then stopped on the camera taping Annamae and Bagel. The little mutt followed her around while she walked around the yard with a basket on her arm.

Picking up last year's old pecans off the ground.

Interesting.

He'd seen her return from her visit to her grandmother and had been curious about how it went. But Annamae had seemed pensive – distracted – when she'd stepped out of her little red car. She'd stared at his home for a good long minute then raced to her carriage house rental as if the hounds of hell were at her feet and he hadn't seen hide nor hair of her for the rest of the weekend. Something was on her mind. Big time.

He should just leave her to her pecan picking.

Should.

But still his feet took him right out the door. She must know she couldn't eat year-old pecans?

The setting sun cast a mellow haze over her as her loosely gathered hair slid to the side every time she picked up another darkened nut.

He leaned back against a tree and waited for her to notice he'd joined her. Except she just kept right on tossing half-rotted nuts into the basket. Her preoccupation and lack of awareness of her surroundings was damned dangerous.

Wynn cleared his throat and said, "Penny for your thoughts."

Annamae bolted upright and dropped the basket on the ground, pecans spilling over into a pile. "Good Lord, Heath. You scared me to pieces." She glanced down at Bagel who wagged his tail in response. "Some watch dog you are."

"You really should be more careful. If I'd been the press,

your photo would be all over the Internet by now." He knelt beside her to help scoop the pecans back into the basket. "You know these nuts are a year old, right?"

She nodded. "I'm collecting shells for mulch and you're right about the need to be more careful. My head's just full with so much going on." Annamae's gaze seemed to turn inward again.

"From coming to Beulah and your visit with your grandmother?" Wynn said gently, trying to bring her back to reality. To the present.

She glanced up quickly, her throat moving in a quick swallow. "Uhm, yes."

He narrowed his eyes. That didn't seem entirely truthful. Was it her ex-fiancé? He couldn't imagine not coming after a beautiful woman like her. "You've been holed up so long in the carriage house, I wasn't sure how it went. Did she have the answers you were looking for?"

She chewed her bottom lip and looked away. "Some."

"What do you plan to do next? Other than be my hide-out tenant."

"Make slug repellant." She smoothed her hair back over her face, and smiled at him.

"Pardon me?" he asked, not following her train of thought, but then that could have something to do with the scent of her soap carrying on the breeze.

Shrugging her shoulders, she gestured to the ground. "Well, all of these pecans on the ground are going to waste and I picked up some literature about all-natural farming at the community garden."

"And you decided you need slug repellant."

"It won't keep the paparazzi away, but it will deter other slimy things. I'm going to plant some flowers around the carriage house. If I have extra mulch, I'll donate it to the community garden." A small smile teased the corners of her mouth upwards. He surveyed her, eyes trailing up and down.

"You don't strike me as the DIY type. You seem too... pampered."

"Now I am insulted. I like being self-sufficient." She stood, basket over her arm. Little Red Riding Hood indeed. "I might even do some baking today. All the apple blossoms put me in the mood for pie. I noticed you have a small patch of strawberries near your house?"

He was feeling hungry himself. But not just for dessert. If they were stuck here together... "I worked hard to grow those. Any pie resulting from my berries should probably be half mine."

Something shifted in her eyes, uncertainty – and aware-ness. Finally she nodded. "Okay. But if you want pie, you have to help me." She thrust the basket at him. "So let's get picking."

ANNAMAE WORKED HER knife faster, channeling all her

pent-up frustrations into hulling the strawberries she'd picked with Heath.

Being productive.

She sat on the opposite side of her kitchen table from Heath. He was more adept than her at hulling. His knife smoothed a circle around the hull, neatly plucking out the leaves too.

Her eyes slid to Heath's strong hands as he worked. All of his movements were even, fluid. There was a confidence to the way that he moved, a sureness that sparked curiosity in her. Hazel's final piece of advice still tingled through Annamae even as she worked to feed at least one hunger – with food. Could she really just indulge in some steaming hot sex? No strings. Quit being the responsible girl and do something just for her?

The possibility enticed her – and scared her all the way to the roots of her freshly dyed hair. She sliced into a strawberry so hard the blade nicked her finger.

She searched for something, anything, to fill the silence and perhaps help her understand why she was drawn to have a completely illogical affair with this man. "What made you decide to become a farmer?"

"What makes you think I wasn't born into the profession?" He arched a dark eyebrow, a sexy twinkle lighting his eyes. "You seemed to enjoy the strawberries well enough."

She couldn't hold back a laugh. "No offense meant, but there aren't many to work with."

"True enough," he admitted. "I'm still learning the business."

"Which brings me back to my original question."

"I needed a change of scenery." The light left his eyes. "Job burnout."

"What did you do before?"

"Well, you're a nosy one," he answered evasively. "Let's talk about your ex-fiancé?"

She knew well tricks to avoiding answering questions. She'd been taught that skill well for interviews. "We can. But you go first. It's not like we have many people to talk to, all locked up and hiding from the press. Or at least I'm hiding," she felt herself starting to babble, "Why don't you ever leave?"

"I'm on the run from the law." His voice was matter-of-fact as he set aside his knife, staring directly at her.

Oh God. Her throat started closing and she couldn't remember where she'd left her inhaler. "Seriously?"

He cracked a smile that traveled up to his eyes. "No, Red. I'm just antisocial. It's as simple as that."

She exhaled slowly. "Then why did you list the carriage house for rent?"

"I didn't. The town likes to interfere under the guise of helping out. They thought I needed the extra cash because the orchard hasn't borne good fruit the last few years." The light came on his eyes again, making those craggy features and tough guy look so approachable.

Charming.

Sexy.

"Uhm." She swallowed hard. "I think we have enough berries for me to cook and I should probably start my mulching project. So, uhm, ..."

"Right." He shoved to his feet. "That's my cue to leave. I can take a hint. You can leave my serving of the pie on the porch. Shoot me a text when it's there."

A text? Just the word made her think of the sad way she and Boone had resorted to communicating, today and over the past weeks. Through text messages rather than human contact.

Watching Heath's broad shoulders as he retreated, she felt such a deep pang of regret she found herself blurting, "How about I bring it by and we eat it together while it's still hot?"

He stopped, his hand on the doorknob and she thought for a second he was going to reject her offer. The brief outline of a smile touched his lips. Then he nodded and said softly, "You asked about my job before ... I majored in psychology in college."

The door closed behind him, leaving her more con-fused – and hungrier – than ever.

WYNN DISHED UP a second helping of the pie and dumped a

scoop of vanilla ice cream on top. After years of eating bachelor food or crappy fare in undercover dives, he'd forgotten how good real home cooking tasted.

Tiger watched from the top of the refrigerator while Bagel slept on a mat by the door. Two more cats purred from under the table. The scene was downright domestic. Normal, yet also alien to a man who'd lived undercover for so much of his career.

He shoveled another bite in his mouth, chewing, then feeling the weight of Annamae's stare from across the table.

"What?" he asked self-consciously.

She smiled, her hair loose around her shoulders now. "I'm just trying to envision you as Sigmund Freud, and it's not meshing for me."

"I didn't say I'm a psychiatrist." He'd turned that psych degree into profiling, with a minor in criminal justice. He'd worked his ass off to get that degree during his days as a street cop.

"Oh, so you're a psychologist? Or a social worker? It's still not fitting for me." She crinkled her nose.

"So you're the kind to stereotype. What about me doesn't fit for you? The shrink part or the college educated part?"

She leaned back, eyes wide. "I think you just insulted me again."

"I'm fairly certain you insulted me this time." His tone was tight, guarded.

"Then I apologize," she said with undeniable sincerity. "But you haven't given me much to go on about yourself."

True enough. And that was for her own protection. "I'm a private person."

"Looks to me like you're a recluse."

"I told you. I'm burned out. My job ... I needed a break." And that was one hundred percent honest. After a year undercover stint busting the Dimitri crime family, he needed time to recharge. He still wasn't sure if maybe he needed a whole new course for his life. The thought scared the hell out of him. So many uncertainties. But he couldn't think about that right now. He just had to make it until the trial.

"People who need a break take a cruise or go to the Florida Keys and get drunk. They don't commit to an orchard." Her gaze was sharp, keen.

"Maybe I'm planning on staying here."

"You plan to support yourself with this? You may want to consider going back to college and study agriculture." She shoveled another piece of pie into her mouth.

She had a point. And she was digging too close, too deep when he was tempted to see what ice cream and berry juice tasted like on her lips.

"Annamae Jessup, you sure are full of questions. Are you sure you're just an actress and not an interrogator?"

"Just an actress?" Her voice arched up. It was almost imperceptible, but he had spent years learning to read the nuances of communication. He knew he had struck a nerve.

"You don't like that label."

"No," she admitted, looking down at her dessert. "Going to college wasn't pretend on the show. I just finished up my degree."

"Congratulations," he said and meant it. He knew how tough it was to work full time and go to school. She also had a wealthy family and could have lived off the family if she chose. "You'll pardon me for having missed your reality show, but I'm not much of one for television. What's your major?"

"Hospitality. Although I have to confess, I'm crushed you're not a fan of the show." She patted her chest and rolled her eyes with overplayed drama, then laughed, a pretty light sound that swirled around the dingy old kitchen.

And lit the dark corners inside him.

Before he could rethink or second guess his actions, he leaned across the table and stroked her hair behind her ear, his knuckles skimming her cheek. God, her skin was soft and warm.

And he was on fire to kiss her.

She didn't pull away. In fact, her pupils widened with an answering desire so he went for it. He pressed his mouth to hers and damn, but the berries tasted even better on her lips, on her tongue. Desire kicked through him and had him standing without breaking contact because yes, she stood too—.

Just as the security system blared.

Chapter Six

T HE SECURITY ALARM jolted Annamae back in her seat, back into the reality of what had just happened. God, she'd just kissed a man she barely knew. And while she wanted to act on all the desire screaming through her from that brief contact, shouldn't she at least sleep on her grandmother's advice for a little longer?

She scraped back her chair, her dog jumping to his paws on full alert. "I guess the press must have gotten through your gates after all."

Heath clasped her arm, his grip firm but gentle. "We can't be so certain it's the media."

"Who else could it be? Oh, maybe a bear I guess, which is almost as scary as a reporter," she joked in hopes of distracting herself from the warmth spreading through her at his touch.

"There are worse things than bears and paparazzi, Red." He guided her toward the stairs and opened a door, Bagel darting inside then back out again. "Stay in here while I check it out."

In here looked a lot like a fallout shelter. Nerves pattered down her spine. "Uhm, I'm not comfortable being shut in there for a number of reasons." She gestured to the gathering darkness of the room. "Like if you're psycho or if the bear eats you and I can't get out and——."

"Fine," he groused, "you and Bagel go in the bathroom. Lock the door. And take your cell phone and keep Bagel quiet if you can."

He thrust her purse into her arms and backed her into the downstairs bathroom before she could blink. Her new pup kept barking and the alarm continued to blare, blare, blare and then....

Silence. Bagel closed his jaws and plopped on his butt, head tipping to the side. Annamae's heart hammered in her ears.

Why was his reaction so over the top? She appreciated that he cared about security, but that room under the stairs had her questioning what was really going on with his seclusion. The town trusted him, everyone she'd spoken to. Her instincts said he was trustworthy but her instincts were seriously in question these days.

Her ribcage went tight with panic. Her throat began to close with an impending asthma attack that had her digging in her purse for her inhaler.

Three deep breaths later, she burst through the door, determined to go back to her place. Except it wasn't her place. Was the retirement home still open? She snapped her fingers for the dog to follow her, glanced back to be sure he'd obeyed, then—

She slammed into a rock hard chest. Gulp.

A rock hard chest that called to her to linger. She averted her eyes from Heath's and took a steadying breath. "If everything's okay now, I'll just go."

"Everything appears to be all right. Just a deer leaping through the grounds and tripping the system. But I can't be sure until I've swept the camera footage of the grounds more thoroughly."

He had cameras that watched the whole grounds? Had he been watching *her*? She'd thought she was safe from that here.

"Well, then, Heath, how about you watch to make sure I get back to the carriage house and then I'll lock myself in?" She scooped up her dog and stepped around the handsome hulk in front of her luring her to think with her hormones instead of her mind. She raced to the back door, calling over her shoulder. "Okay? Or maybe I'll see my grandma or—"

"Annamae." He palmed the doorframe. "I am not a criminal."

"Of course you're not. I know that. You're just worried about security." She looked at the panel he'd opened, full of security screens and shivered. Annamae paused, forcing lightness into her features. "Maybe you're a secret millionaire or deposed prince or whatever. I'm the last one to dig into anybody's privacy." She yanked the door open and stepped out onto the porch.

"Listen to me. You need to stop." He put a hand on her shoulder, the moon and floodlights beaming down. "I'm not wealthy. And I'm not royalty. I'm a cop."

WYNN WAITED FOR her to respond, scanning the property. He'd turned on the floodlights to be sure he could keep an eye on things while making certain she didn't sprint off, freaked out that he might be a serial killer. So, eyes on the grounds, he waited for Annamae's reaction to his declaration.

He didn't have to wait long.

She laughed. Hard. So hard she sagged back against the door and her dog looked at her like she was crazy. And indeed, there was a hint of hysteria in her laughter.

"What's so damn funny?" Wynn asked.

She wiped a wrist across her eyes. "You're the least cop looking guy I've ever met. You wouldn't make it past the first casting call."

Fair enough. "That's what being undercover is all about."

"Undercover?"

"I'm trusting you with a lot here." He lowered his voice, nerves still on edge from the alarm. Of course trust was easy when he'd had her investigated and technically she couldn't leave the grounds unless he let her. But then that would be kidnapping, which clearly she'd thought him capable of two minutes ago. "I am an undercover police detective keeping a low profile until some heat blows over."

"Why should I believe you?"

"Why would I lie?"

She studied him for a moment, her sharp eyes taking him all in. He felt the pull of attraction to her again as he met her gaze. The corners of her mouth faintly pulled upwards. A nervous half-smile played on her lips. "To lure me back inside to kill me and stuff my body into a freezer?"

Just from her flippant answer he could tell she was relaxing. Trusting.

"Let's sit out here on the porch, out in the open, and do some Googling."

"Uhm, Googling?"

"You'll see." He dropped down on the bench, leaving a space free beside him, while making sure he could still access the gun tucked under his loose shirt over his t-shirt. He pulled out his phone and launched Google, the sound of night bugs mingling with the tones of his phone.

She chewed her bottom lip, then sat slowly. "Okay, it's not like I could actually make a run for it if you're truly a psycho."

"A ringing endorsement of my character. Thanks. But if I'd wanted to kill you, you never would have made it out the front door. Lucky for you, I'm completely legit." He passed her his phone. Complete with an article about the Dimitri bust.

Her brow furrowed, her eyes moving as she read. "This

Wynn Rafferty, the policeman who solved the case but lost his partner. You're his partner and you're not really dead?"

His chest burned with memories of how fast that day had gone to hell. He kept an eye on the property in front of him, alert to any movements.

"I'm Wynn Rafferty."

"You've even been lying about your name, *Heath Lambert?*"

"I'm trusting you right now, a woman I only just met." He took his phone back to thumb through photos about the story until one landed on an image of his face, an earlier photo of him wearing his uniform. "Probably the stupidest thing I've ever done."

"Then why are you doing it?" She looked up at him, her cheek close to his shoulder. Her scent a light sweetness in his nose that made him want to bend closer.

"Because I hate the fear I just saw in your eyes. I've worked my whole life to protect people from feeling that way."

He held the edge of the phone until she took it from him, her gaze dropping to the article detailing the bust on the Dimitri drug syndicate. How during that bust a couple of kids from the local high school had shown up to try and bring their friend out of the gang. One of those teens got shot and killed by Dimitri himself—a teen Wynn knew from his earlier work at a rec center. To this day he blamed himself for that kid's death. For that instant when the youth looked at him and recognition lit in the boy's eyes. How damn tragic that in trying to save the kid through working at the rec center, he'd ultimately caused the youth's death. The boy had followed in his footsteps, trying to save others.

Wynn rubbed his forehead, pressing against an ache that never went away. "I'll just be glad when the trial is over and life can return to normal."

Or something like normal. He had no idea what that meant for him, but the thought of returning to his work in Miami turned him cold.

She tapped the edge of his phone. "I remember this case."

God, he sure as hell would never forget. "The Dimitri family connection made the headlines—they have friends in high places. Guess you and I are both well known in our own way."

Except all she'd done was bail on a celebrity marriage. He'd failed to save a good kid who'd put himself at risk to help a friend. He'd spent a lot of time thinking about that day and what he might have done differently. For the life of him, he couldn't come up with a scenario that would have resulted in the boy walking away. But even if he'd excised some of the guilt, he still felt humbled by the way the kid had put himself on the line for a friend.

Antony Marks had a sense of purpose. A rock-solid moral compass that was rare to find in one so young. After years of undercover work where right and wrong only came in shades of gray, Wynn found a lot to admire in that.

"That's why you've been staying in rural Alabama. So no one will see you before the trial." Annamae peered up at him from the phone, eyes roaming his face as if testing it for signs of the man he'd once been in that pressed uniform. "No one recognizes you here so far from home."

He hardly knew himself anymore, either. He sure did recognize attraction though. And this hunger for Annamae wasn't going away anytime soon. Her slow, thorough perusal of him amped up the heat he'd been trying to ignore.

"Short of plastic surgery, there's not much I could have done to hide in Miami unless I locked myself in a hotel room for the year. It's taken the justice system months to crank the trial up on the docket with the Dimitri family lawyers filing continuances every damn day. I couldn't live that way and didn't want to put a protective detail at risk, especially for that length of time."

Enough lives had been lost to Dimitri family ruthlessness. They'd brought a new, effective business model with them from a global drug trade, their wealth and connections providing a protective veneer and plenty of champions among the rich and famous. They would defend Serge Dimitri with everything they had.

"Still, wouldn't they consider the work worth their while to make sure you're safe to nail this guy?" Annamae kept her focus on the case, her sharp mind working through the details in a way that impressed him.

"I have been safe."

"So safe I got through the front gate," she pointed out, arching a brow at him.

"You're ... unexpected." Something about her had gotten under his guard before she even opened her mouth when he'd seen her at his front gate that first time. He touched her chin lightly, thinking about their kiss earlier.

"Me?" A grin stole over her features. "I think that may be the nicest compliment anyone has ever paid me."

"How so?" He stroked her jaw lightly before his hand slid away again.

"I've always been the normal one, the beige backdrop to my flamboyant sisters." She laughed lightly, touching her head, "Although maybe my ever-changing hair color isn't so beige anymore."

"It's not your hair that draws me." He wondered how anyone could see her as ordinary. Everything about her sparkled with energy, intelligence. Vibrancy.

"Clearly, my hair wouldn't," she muttered self-consciously.

He clasped her wrist. "You don't need to say things like that."

"I'm not looking for compliments." She went very still under his touch.

He loosened his hold, his thumb caressing the inside of her wrist.

"I know." He stroked up her arm, his hand learning the

feel of her as he skimmed a touch up to her face again. "It's your eyes. They've drawn me from the start. Not wise for a man in my position."

But right now, with his nerves raw and his libido on overdrive, he couldn't find the will to resist.

HAVE A FLING, Annamae.

She didn't want her grandmother's voice in her head right now. Not when Heath—that is, *Wynn*—looked at her like she was even more appealing than the strawberry pie she'd made. Yet she kept remembering Hazel Mae's matter-of-fact prescription for getting over a bad breakup. Have a fling!

"What are we doing?" she heard herself ask, then winced since she sounded incredibly clueless. "I mean—I know where this is going. But—"

"I know what I want." Wynn's hands moved to her shoulders. "I'm one hundred percent clear on that. But I should make a run around the perimeter of the fences. Scan the camera feeds just to be safe. That'll give you enough time to decide if we want the same thing."

She opened her mouth then realized she had no idea what to say to that. She closed it again.

"But would you consider giving me five minutes to persuade the outcome of your decision before I go?" His palm shifted so he cupped her chin, his thumb running along her lower lip in a way that inspired wicked, carnal thoughts.

Her eyes fluttered for a moment before she realized how easily she played into his hands. Instead, she gave his thumb a bite.

His dark laugh didn't sound at all deterred. "That works, too."

Her cheeks burned. "I have no idea what you mean."

"I hope you're here when I get back, Annamae. I can't wait to find out what a lie you've been living with this whole good girl, beige thing."

He strode away before she'd even caught her breath, the taste of his thumb still salty on her tongue.

Bagel barked at him as left, as if asking him to come back. If Annamae weren't careful, she'd be panting after him soon too.

Oh wait, she already was.

Her heartbeat pounded. She couldn't take a steady breath—and it didn't have jack to do with her asthma. All this heady sexual hunger had Wynn Rafferty's name written on it. Her eyes ate him up even now as he vanished into the barn to retrieve his truck.

Had she been living a lie as the good girl?

She knew he'd been teasing her and yet, in a lot of ways, she had. She'd taken her role so seriously, she'd let it dictate her life, her choices. And she'd been sleepwalking through her life for so long she hadn't even noticed. Wynn was giving her a chance to make this decision for herself, so she wasn't going to play the scene just for the hell of it. She would choose.

And she wanted him.

Not because her grandmother said she should have a fling or because she'd realized that she and Boone hadn't loved each other enough. She would sleep with Wynn because she was wildly attracted to him. Because being with him made her feel a quivery excitement she'd never experienced before. And possibly even because she was a little bit her father's daughter after all.

An adventurer.

Rising out of her chair, she went back inside the house. She pulled the hair tie out of her topknot and freed the newly colored caramel strands, the hue closer to her natural color than anything she'd worn in years. While Bagel made himself comfortable among the cats in the living room, Annamae took the stairs up to Wynn's bedroom.

Slow. Deliberate. With purpose.

"I am having an affair, tonight," she told the black and white kitten she found curled on a crisply made bed.

The kitten sat up at this news, folding her tail neatly around her feet as she seemed to listen.

"I know," Annamae replied like they were old friends. "Phone the press, right? But could use a throwaway phone so they don't show up and climb those apple trees with a telephoto lens?" She ran a hand over the gray quilt folded at the end of the California king-sized mattress propped on a simple platform. The only other furniture in the room was a nightstand, bare of anything save a lamp and a book about grafting heirloom fruit trees.

"Mew?" The kitten's conversational skills were better than most of her stepsisters' who'd never been terribly concerned with Annamae's life.

In their defense, she'd never told them she was about to have a torrid affair, so maybe that was an unfair comparison.

"How many cats does the man have?" she wondered, peering under the bed to see if there were any more felines hidden away.

Maybe the kitten was incensed, because she jumped down from the bed and skittered out the door in a hurry, her paws slipping a little on the hardwood floor as she left.

She settled in to read about tree grafting, a topic sure to settle her nerves, if not put her to sleep. But it was actually more interesting than she'd imagined. Wynn had flagged pages about disease-resistant varieties, in keeping with his organic approach to farming. Maybe he could use some pecan mulch...

She wasn't sure how much time had passed when the stairs creaked in the hallway.

"Wynn?" She bolted upright.

The creaking on the stairs stopped.

Panic gripped her.

"What if it wasn't?" a familiar voice asked, as the creaking continued. He stood in the threshold of the bedroom then, studying her as he leaned a shoulder into the doorjamb. "What if I was a hired gun sent to take out anyone in the house?"

"Then I'd be very disappointed in my watch dog who never barked when the door opened downstairs." She set aside the book. "Welcome home, by the way."

His eyes flared with heat. "It is a hell of a welcome, I have to say. When I didn't see you downstairs I thought…"

Her pulse fluttered with nerves. Or maybe it was just anticipation.

"You thought I'd chickened out." She felt brave that she hadn't. She also liked that she'd surprised him. In a good way.

"Before I left, you asked me what we were doing," he reminded her. "You looked a little spooked."

She wondered why he still stood in the doorway. Why he hadn't come closer. Touched her.

By now, she was really, really ready for him to touch her.

"I'm not now." She remembered that he'd wanted her to think this through. To be sure. "And you're right… I'm not nearly as beige as I thought."

One second he stood in the doorway. The next he loomed over her, inches from the bed. He tipped her chin up to see her eyes, studying her.

"You're sure about this happening between us. Now. Tonight." It wasn't a question. That crooked grin of his tipped his lips in a half-smile.

"Didn't I say as much?" Her heart pounded harder at his touch. His nearness. She tipped her cheek so that he touched more of her.

Then, wanting even more, she rose up on her knees so she was almost eye-to-eye with him where he stood beside the bed. The warmth of his hard body beckoned.

"I think country living is turning you sassy, Ms. Jessup." He stroked a finger down the length of her neck, pausing in the hollow at the base of her throat where her pulse did a crazy dance.

"It's not easy holding my own with a surly landlord looking for any excuse to toss me out on my ear." She had to steady herself with a palm against his chest.

She was gratified to feel that his heart slugged a fast pace too.

"Yet you have the power to put an end to all the surliness." He leaned closer, the heat and earthy smell of him reaching out to her.

Her breasts grazed his chest with delectable friction.

"Do tell," she urged, her voice whispered now that their lips were mere inches apart.

"It'll be better if I show you." His hand slid around the back of her neck, pulling her to him.

She had a brief impression of his hungry eyes and then his mouth claimed hers.

And Annamae spontaneously combusted. In a good way.

Heat radiated through her, burning her inside and out. Wynn held her where he wanted her, guiding her where he wanted her and she loved it. Loved how her body answered his like they'd been communicating this way for years instead of moments. No awkwardness. No worry if she was doing something right. This kiss didn't ask questions. It answered them.

Her arms wound around his neck, drawing him down to her. On to the bed. On top of her. The hard, heavy weight of his body sinking into the cradle of hers felt like a homecoming. Like he belonged exactly there. A long sigh hissed between her teeth, the pleasure so sharp and sudden she didn't know what to do with it all.

Then his hands were in her hair, sifting, sinking. Annamae closed her eyes to shut out some of the sensations overwhelming her, needing to anchor herself in the moment before she floated right away on a wave of pleasure. She'd pick through what it all meant later. Right now it was just her lips on his. Her breasts flattened against his chest. The hard length of him pressing against the fly of his jeans to tease her thighs.

His arms banded around her and she felt like a part of him already, and they hadn't even taken their clothes off. As if she could lose herself in this. Him. It was scary and incredible at the same time.

"Clothes off," she murmured against his mouth. Needing to take this feeling to its explosive conclusion.

That was the problem with scary, incredible things. As much as she wanted to savor it, the suspense about how it would all turned out was killing her.

"I knew you were going to be a wild woman in bed." He shifted his kiss from her lips to her neck and then lower, his hands skimming her t-shirt up and off so there was nothing between his lips and her breasts but a kind of exotic Italian lace bra from her mother's European negligee shopping jaunt last season.

Wynn made it clear he was only interested in what lay beneath it, however, his fingers working the clasp as if her barely B-cups were something to write home about. Expensive lace cast aside, he drew the tip of one breast in his mouth, making her toes curl and pleasure coil between her legs.

Some of that scary feeling slipped away as she realized Wynn knew exactly how to take them where she wanted to go. This night wasn't going to end in quiet contentment. It would end in fireworks.

With restless hands, she scraped at his tee, tugging and shoving cotton aside until he leaned up to pull it off for her. By the light of the moon streaming bright through the windows, she got an eyeful of naked broad shoulders and flat pectoral muscles. Abs that made her breath catch.

"Pants too," she blurted, enjoying the show. "I mean, as long as you're at it."

"You make a sexy voyeur." He worked the buttons on his

jeans and shucked them faster than she'd ever have managed. His boxers disappeared too. "But if you keep looking at me like that, Annamae, I'm not going to last long." He reached for her. "Did I mention I've been in hiding for the past year?"

"You mean no women?" Her eyes seemed stuck to him, refusing to obey when she was ready to stop ogling.

He was just so… *So*.

Everything about him was delicious.

"No women." He pulled her up to stand beside him and her eyes still wouldn't behave. He tugged off her jeans and tossed them onto the hardwood floor.

"So all these greedy looks haven't been about me. You're just starved for sex?" she teased.

"First of all, I'm not alone in the greedy looks department." He nipped her ear and slid a hand around her waist, palming the small of her back. "Second, this is all about you. Only you."

He pressed his hips to hers and she was already seeing stars.

She held tight to his shoulders, losing herself in another mind-drugging kiss. He whispered things in her ear. Naughty, hot things that should have made her blush but only made her whimper with need for more.

By the time he slid a finger inside her, she was so revved up she came instantly. Instantly. It was the most insane thing ever. Until he took her in his mouth and made her fly apart all over again. She would have used the last of her strength to straddle him and take what she wanted most, but he must have read her mind because he rolled her on top of him and handed her a condom.

Mindless with want, she simply followed the silent command and took him inside her.

She could have moved against him like a mad woman, but when she saw the sweat bead along his forehead, she knew he hadn't been kidding about not having been with anyone for a while. She let him control the pace, humbled to be the one he chose after all that time.

Just when she thought the night didn't have the power to surprise her anymore, she was most struck by that tender sentiment—that this was more than just a fling because he'd chosen her. The notion got under her skin and into her head until she wanted to hold him all night long and kiss every square inch of him.

He took his time, holding back, finding ways to drive the pleasure higher for her even though he teetered too close to the edge. In the end, she pushed him over, nipping his ear and whispering a precise description of what she planned to do to him the next time she got him naked.

She couldn't savor the victory too long though. The feel of him throbbing deep inside her nudged her into a third orgasm she never would have dreamed possible in one night.

Fireworks, for sure.

She smiled as the aftershocks pulsed along her skin for

long minutes afterward. She couldn't speak. Could barely move. Instead, she just curled up against him and absorbed the warm feel of his chest beneath her cheek.

"Definitely unexpected." His words made her smile right before she might have drifted off.

"You can't have any morning-after regrets yet," she informed him, only half joking. "I'm still in the afterglow stage."

"I'm a guy. We never regret sex." His hand curled around her shoulder, brushing lightly.

She laughed. "Right. Don't know what I was thinking."

Although she did, of course. She was worried he'd regret being with her. He'd be leaving Beulah soon for his trial. And she'd be…

She wasn't even sure.

"I can hear you thinking." He kissed the top of her head, a gentle press of his lips in her hair.

"Is that a crack on me for being an actress? Nothing but air between my ears?"

"Hell no." He shifted her so they lay side by side on the pillow, facing each other. "That's the psych major talking. You went all silent after you said you didn't know what you were thinking—."

"So you assumed I was suddenly thinking deep thoughts." Who knew she was so predictable? Her grandmother had been right. She really wasn't a very good actress.

"Bingo." He lifted a strand of her hair where it lay between them. Stroked it between his thumb and forefinger. "It's only normal, you know. You went from thinking I was some random good old boy farmer to finding out I'm law enforcement, to finding out I'm wildly attracted to you all in one day. Any woman would be overwhelmed."

She knew he was making a joke, but she really did feel kind of undone by the last few days.

"I think I'm just punch drunk from all those orgasms." She deflected the more serious part of the conversation, truly savoring the afterglow. She could live off those endorphins for months.

"Good to know. I hear there's an unlimited supply when you sleep in this bed." Carefully, he smoothed the strands of her hair back into place. "Red, I want you to know I'm going to keep you safe."

Had she thought she'd deflected the more serious part of this conversation?

"I'm not worried. I feel safer here than just walking around Atlanta on any given day."

"I mean from the Dimitris. From the trial hanging over my head. If it comes down to it, and I think it's not safe for you here, I'll make sure you get protection somewhere else."

"I don't want to be anywhere else." Could he do that? Send her away if he was worried about her? As a law enforcement officer, maybe he could.

"All the stories that ran in the paper... they made me sound like I screwed up that op."

She pressed a palm to his chest over his heartbeat. "No they didn't."

"Yeah, they did. They talked about the teen – Antony – who got caught in the crossfire of police ready to make a bust, but it was a cop from some other unit who jumped the gun. We'd been paired up for weeks, both working the same undercover operation—neither of us wanting to compromise our cases. It's not like on TV where you can just pull rank and get rid of a guy when you feel like he's not quite up to snuff. There's so much time invested, lives at stake if covers get blown. You're living in this elaborate web of lies. It's... complicated."

She heard something different in his voice. Something personal. He'd spent a lot of time thinking about this—she didn't need a psych degree to know it.

"I thought the news coverage made it sound like that teen was in the wrong place at the wrong time. Just bad timing. He went to try and talk his friend out of leaving a gang—"

His face was strained, taking on five years' worth of lines in an instant. "He was a great kid. Antony. He'd been a runner in another crew when he was younger, had a long rap sheet he did earn, but he got out. Really worked his ass off to stay out of that bad element. He didn't recognize me when I was working undercover, but I knew him from when I'd worked in Ft. Lauderdale. I helped him clean up when he hung out at a rec center where I volunteered."

"So you saved him from street violence once, only to see him die the way so many gang members do." She couldn't imagine how hard his job must be. How painful it must be to watch a life end that way, especially a young person full of such promise. "I'm so sorry."

"Right before he died, though, he recognized me." The rawness in his voice made her throat close up.

"Did he say anything?"

He shook his head. "No. There was just that—light of recognition. And... I don't know. I swear there was a peace in his eyes. I've thought about that moment so many times, knowing that I might have read into it what I wanted to see."

He shrugged. Like he had more to say but changed his mind.

She held his hand. Kissed his cheek. "You know what you saw. Some people are born knowing exactly who they are. Maybe that boy felt a peace because he died doing something he believed in."

Annamae didn't know if it was the right thing to say. If it gave him any comfort. But he lifted their twined hands and kissed the back of hers. "Thank you."

"I hope your testimony puts away the person who killed Antony." She understood a little better why he'd given a year of his life to staying in hiding while the government built their case. It was about more than drugs or a job. It was about justice for a young man taken too soon.

"It will, Red. I know it."

They lay together in silence for a long time, and she felt his breathing go even. Her mind was unsettled though, her afterglow chased off by criminals gunning for Wynn. What a dark world she'd stumbled into. She must have looked like something out of a cartoon with her red convertible and her dog and bleached blonde hair when she'd barreled up to his gate. No wonder he hadn't wanted any part of her on his property.

She would never forgive herself if she'd endangered him. Or the case that meant so much to him. Which was why she needed to play by his rules, be discreet. And leave when he told her to.

She just hoped she wouldn't leave too big of a piece of her heart behind when that day came.

When Wynn's cell phone buzzed on the nightstand by her ear, she realized she must have fallen asleep too. Disoriented, she blinked in the darkness, but Wynn was alert instantly, his face illuminated by the phone.

"Hello?" His eyes went to her even as he fielded the call.

She liked that. Liked the connection. Wynn must have seen who it was on caller ID because he switched the call to speaker phone so she could hear.

"Mr. Lambert, it's Gus Fields from the service station near the Sleep Tight Motor Lodge. I had a customer out here earlier tonight asking about that starlet. Ms. Jessup? She was real persistent-like."

Annamae sat up, dragging the sheet with her. Who was

asking about her? A reporter?

"What did you say?" Wynn slid out of the blankets, putting his feet on the floor.

Confused, Annamae wondered what time it was. Where was he going?

"I didn't tell her anything, like we agreed. But Roofus Haverty has a mouth on him like an old woman."

Annamae frowned, not appreciating that comparison.

"What did Roofus say?"

"He went and told the lady how Ms. Jessup went to your place one time. And this woman—kinda uppity like—she lit out of here a little while ago. Just now, Roofus told me she was asking for directions to your place. I woulda called sooner but I got busy—."

"It's okay, Gus. I appreciate the—"

The security alarm blared.

Chapter Seven

WYNN TOSSED ANNAMAE her phone. Her real phone this time. Not a throwaway.

"Take this, get dressed and get into the room I showed you. It's safe in there. You can watch what happens on the screens."

Her movements were shaky, but she was already in her t-shirt.

"Do you know how to get in there? Will I be able to get back out?"

"Yes to both." His tone was even, but the lines on his face had reappeared. He pocketed his phone and checked the clip on his 9mm. "Take Bagel with you."

"It's probably just someone from the media." Annamae wrapped a blanket around her shoulders and followed him downstairs, the rest of her clothes tucked under her arm. "Right?"

"Probably." He ground his teeth together. Hoped like hell it was just someone looking for Annamae and not him.

And if they were looking for Annamae to get to him? Wynn's brain blanked like a TV channel that wouldn't come in.

"Be safe," she told him, kissing him on his cheek and catching him off guard with the unexpected tenderness.

When had anyone ever looked out for him?

Even his partner had been trying to make the big bust, risking his ass to make the collar and not to protect their cover. And that guy had gotten *paid* to protect Wynn.

"You too." He gave her a gentle shove into the safe room, stepping behind her to check the security cameras for a direction to go in.

Both their eyes went to the wall of video screens to see a woman in a white BMW and a pink short sleeve suit at the back entrance of the farm.

"Oh God." Annamae gripped the wall. "It's my mom."

"Your mother?" Wynn swore while he shut off the alarm. "Where is the camera entourage? I thought your family normally travelled with a photo crew."

He checked all the other cameras. Pressed a button for more angles on each, sweeping the road and the rows of trees.

"I don't see Josephine—the woman who usual tapes my mother's scenes." Annamae shook her head, her hair tangled all around her, looking so damn sexy, so damn perfect. "Mom hasn't gone anywhere by herself in years."

"It's your call as to what happens next. Do I let her in and risk her telling someone where you are? Or do you want to go out and convince her to go away?" He knew that wasn't really a choice. Annamae could get hurt if she went out there and the gates were being watched. "Never mind. I'll go get her."

"I've had my cell turned off. I swear." She showed him, her hand shaking. "She's probably been calling. I could phone her and let her know I'm okay. She doesn't have to come inside the gate."

"No. Keep the phone off. It's better not to risk it." He backed out of the safe room. "I'll be back with her soon."

Annamae nodded, the furrow deepening between her brows as she picked up Bagel to keep her vigil over the video feeds.

Jogging out of the house and leaping into the truck, Wynn hoped he wasn't screwing up left and right. Less than a month to go before his court date and all hell was breaking loose here on this supposedly secluded farm.

But not for the world would he trade meeting Annamae.

The realization came like a back slap rather than any cool-headed rationalization. It was true though. He'd risk his own neck before going back to a life without her.

What scared him was the thought that he could be risking hers.

Jamming on the gas, he drove like a demon to the back gate and hoped Mrs. Jessup would prove reasonable.

She didn't look reasonable when he pulled up in his truck. Sure, her pressed suit and neat blonde chignon were both perfect and her white Beemer didn't have a spot on it despite the Alabama spring mud season. But the expression on her face screamed that Beulah, Alabama was the last place she wanted to be right now, especially facing down a rusty fence that combined chicken wire and barbed wire into the perfect redneck answer to Alcatraz.

"Mrs. Jessup?" he called, parking the truck across the fence from her car.

"Who are you?" Her eyes narrowed in a fair imitation of her daughter when Annamae was riled. Except the elder version didn't look like she'd ever hulled a strawberry or snuggled a mutt. "And how do you know who I am?"

Wynn kept an eye out for movements in his peripheral vision, praying that no more of Annamae's family would be tracking her down.

"I'm a friend of your daughter's. Would you mind getting in the car and following me inside once I open the gate?" He didn't want the BMW sitting out here where someone might see it and make the connection that Beulah's local runaway celebrity was staying with him.

Annamae's whereabouts were strictly conjecture. Wynn had deliberately planted a few rumors with townspeople to see what ideas took hold.

"I most certainly will not. Do you know where my daughter is, young man?" She drew herself up to her full height, which might have been five foot four at the most. "I will call the local sheriff—."

"Last chance if you want me to open the gate, ma'am."

He held the remote control in his hand and flashed it her way so she could see what he had. "I'll hit the button if you get in the car so you can drive through."

The glare she gave him would have frozen some men. Damn, but he hoped she wasn't serious about calling the sheriff. That would blow the lid right off the low profile plan.

"You must know the last thing your daughter wants is more drama," he reminded her, hoping the woman had a heart under that icy veneer.

"You think you know my daughter?" she shot back, stalking over to the BMW and opening the driver's side door. "I assure you, the rest of Atlanta thought they did too, and Annamae proved them all wrong. So whatever you think you know about her… you don't."

She sounded so damn sure he couldn't decide if the woman knew something he didn't, or if she was the true actress in the family.

The reality TV matriarch got into her expensive car and turned on the ignition. True to his word, Wynn opened the gate and let her drive through before he shut it. He had no idea what the plan was from here other than to get her back to the house to see Annamae. But he didn't want her leaving his property to spread the word of her daughter's whereabouts.

Then again, what guy wanted to play host to the mother of the red-hot woman he'd just started sleeping with?

Of course, those concerns were minor compared to both women's safety. But he didn't like this. And he knew her arrival spelled trouble.

"LET ME BE sure I'm clear on this." Delilah Jessup ignored the cup of tea that Annamae had set in front of her back at the carriage house half an hour later. "You traded a life of wealth, love and security for an apple farmer?"

Bagel paced back and forth at her mother's feet, still incensed at having to part company with the cats over at Wynn's. Annamae, for that matter, was kind of incensed at having to part company with Wynn, but maybe it was just as well she took a little time to figure out what was happening between them before she did something crazy. Like fall for a cop hiding out as a fruit farmer.

He'd needed to check in with an outside security company though, admitting that he was bringing in extra help to get through these last weeks before the trial. She'd figured coming back to the carriage house would keep her mom out of his way and raise fewer questions about their relationship. But Delilah Jessup missed nothing.

"I didn't make any trades, Mom." No wonder she'd gravitated toward a life of beige. There were just too many damn colorful personalities in her family. Annamae got lost around them. "I broke off my engagement with Boone because he and I are not right for each other. We were getting married for the wrong reasons."

"Which all of Atlanta knows now, thanks to that stunt with the radio show. *Sex Talk with Serena*? Honestly, Annamae, I'm not sure what came over you to make your plan to bolt so very public."

Seriously? Everything our family did was public.

But pointing that out to her mother wouldn't accomplish anything. And who knows, maybe calling the radio show hadn't been an accident. Perhaps some part of her was so used to the reality show life that she'd subconsciously taken the easy way out. She'd done what she'd been doing for years – using broadcasting to document her life, good and bad.

The thought that she'd hurt Boone that way even accidentally on purpose stung. A lot.

Annamae wrapped her arms around herself. "Did you follow me all the way here to chew me out, Mom? Because I came here to get away from the censure and the opinions of my family 24-7." She stood, desperate to get away from this conversation with her mother. "You realize that's all *Acting Up* ever was? An excuse to see a wealthy family nitpick each other and catfight with their friends?"

She wanted no part of that anymore. And she needed to make sure she didn't allow herself any more radio show style subliminal slip-ups.

"Sweetie, you can't deny that we lead a life of privilege

most people only dream about." She twisted her wedding ring set front and center, highlighting the obscene amount of carats on her finger. "I know you've never been dazzled by the money, but having lived with it and without it, I can tell you it's a hell of a lot easier *with*."

"You didn't ask me what I wanted when you made that choice for both of us." Annamae thought about what Hazel Mae had shared with her—the fact that her father had wanted to keep her, had wanted to give her a whole different life. "So pardon me if I don't ask you for your opinion when it's my turn to decide how to live my life. I've lived with the cameras and without them, and I would give up a whole lot of our lifestyle to spend some time *without*."

"My God. You spend a few days in Beulah and you're turning into me." Her mother squeezed her temples. "Would you look in my purse for my migraine medicine? Or do you have a bottle of wine? That might help."

"No wine." Technically a lie because there was some apple cider wine in the cabinet, but it was too early for that, and the last thing any of them needed was her mother getting sloppy drunk, spilling secrets and mascara—tinged tears all over everything. Annamae took her mother's bright pink handbag that she'd ordered from a designer in Paris after a couture show just a few weeks ago. The bag was gorgeous, the price tag ridiculous. And she still couldn't understand why people wanted to watch her family buy stupid things like designer purses. "Here are your pills though."

"Thank you." Shaking out two into her hand, her mother downed the medicine with a sip of tea, then sagged back with a melodramatic sigh.

Annamae chewed her bottom lip, knowing she should just walk out but somehow, she found herself staying. Asking. "What do you mean that I've turned into you?" She'd always considered her and her mother polar opposites. "You said it yourself, you'd choose security over adventure every time."

"Not every time, darling, or you wouldn't be here." Her mother winked at her over the rim of the teacup. "Will you tell that little dog to settle? He's making me nervous."

"You're making him nervous, Mom." She scooped Bagel up. He had refused to settle, unable to find a good spot on his favorite couch crowded with all their company. Besides that, she shook her toe in a twitchy rhythm, keeping Bagel in a constant state of readiness for her to get up. "Sit still."

"I can't believe you got a dog with your asthma." Hazel Mae sniffed, drumming the side of the teacup with finely manicured fingers.

"I've always wanted a dog and he doesn't bother my asthma in the least. Actually, I've never felt healthier than since I came to stay out here." She settled back in the chair across from her mom, trying to see herself in the primped and coiffed perfection that was Delilah.

Well, perfect aside from the migraines, drinking tendencies, and probable eating disorder that kept her too thin.

"Anyway, I fell for a charismatic man once, Annamae, and I nearly turned my life inside out for him." She shook her head, her eyes seeing another time as she stared out the window. "Love and lust—and it was a fair amount of both—can make a woman foolish. He wanted to hunt alligators, for crying out loud. In the bush. I'm not sure that farming apples in Beulah is going to lead to much more happiness."

"We only just met," Annamae reminded her, although the conversation was hitting close to home. Especially the lust part. "We're not talking about a future."

"Right. But dumping a star athlete and running away from home aren't like you, so I'm not going to leave it to chance that you'll make the right choice where this Heath Lambert character is concerned."

Delilah's eyes narrowed, her voice bellowing with practiced stage drama. Acting even without the presence of the cameras. "How on earth did you meet him? I think you're lying to me and he's the real reason you broke up with Boone."

What would her mother say if she knew he wasn't a struggling apple farmer, but a decorated police detective? Not that she could even trust her mother with the information. If her mom caught a whiff of the sense that Heath was Wynn and Wynn was already newsworthy, her mother would run with that story to save face. She would spin it into some new tale about her daughter falling for a man in blue.

She had to throw her mother off the scent.

"You sound like a tabloid, Mom," Annamae informed her flatly. "Heath is just a nice, regular guy. And he's helping me keep a low profile while I figure things out."

They hadn't had time to come up with a plan for what to tell her mother, so she figured it was best to stay hazy on the details for now. Later, once she got her mother settled, she'd go back over to Wynn's and figure out what to do next.

"Hmm." She kept drinking her tea, eying Annamae like she was waiting for her to break and spill her guts.

Might as well offer her some real meat to chew on. "Besides, you ought to know the real reason I came to Beulah was to find Grandma."

The teacup slipped a bit in her hand. Tea spilled on the pink suit. Annamae leaped up to get a towel while her mother righted the cup and set it on a nearby end table. "You can't be serious."

"Why else would I come here?" And that was the truth.

Her mother shrugged. "I really assumed it was for the sexy apple farmer."

"I only met the apple farmer because I wanted to find out about my roots. To meet Hazel Mae." Her mother didn't need to know the rest about Heath/Wynn.

Her mom eyed her warily. "And have you spoken with her?"

"Yes, I have. More than once."

"You did this to hurt me, didn't you? You wanted to lash

out at me and now you have." Her mother dabbed at the drying tea stains as if she could blot the stain of her daughter's betrayal out of her life.

"Mother? Mother! Stop. Listen to me, please." She clasped her wrist. "This isn't about you. This is about me and what *I* need."

"What do you need that I didn't give you?"

How could she put this diplomatically, especially in light of how the new things she'd learned about her mom? Thanks to her grandmother, she had a whole different view of her mother. Her father. Herself. She struggled for honest words and they came out half choked on tears. "I feel cheated I didn't get to meet her before now."

"She had a choice." Her mother straightened in her seat, all pretense of ladylike demeanor gone as she pointed an accusatory finger. "She sided with her globetrotting son when he sailed off into the sunset without us."

"I think she has regrets about that decision," Annamae said gently.

"She ought to regret it! If she'd sided with me, maybe he and I could have—" She stopped herself. Crossed her legs again. "But that's all water under the bridge. Annamae, I did my best. And your adoptive father loves you very much."

"Does he?" She'd longed for that sense of family her whole life and never felt it. No matter how hard she tried to make a place for herself with the Jessups, she simply was not one of them. Didn't matter what name they gave her. "I appreciate that he gave me a home and a name, Mom. But I don't think he's ever felt a personal attachment to me."

It felt liberating to say it aloud. She'd been afraid of that simple truth for so long, but once spoken aloud, it had less power to hurt her. Perhaps because she knew somewhere out there, her real father had wanted her. At least a little.

For a time.

Her mother's lips went thin, her pink lipstick smudged. Unusual. But she hadn't had access to her makeup technician today. "I drove all this way to talk some sense into you, only to find you completely brainwashed against me by a senile old woman."

"All this way? It's less than three hours, Mom. If you leave now you can be home for lunch." Even as she said it, she knew that wasn't really an option.

Wynn might not let her mother leave until after the trial. He hadn't said as much, but if she posed a risk to their security, she wouldn't be surprised. All the Jessup money wouldn't sway him. She'd seen his commitment to his job and his passion about prosecuting the Dimitri family when he'd told her the truth about his identity.

"Don't be silly. I didn't get any sleep last night, so I need a nap." She stood, smoothing the crisp fabric of her pink pencil skirt. "But after that, you and I are going to have a little talk with your grandmother so we can chase the ghosts out of the family closet for once and for all."

"IF THE DIMITRI family is making a move, they're hiding it well."

The words on the other end of the phone didn't assure Wynn in the least.

Sun baking through the windshield, he sat in his truck in the middle of his farm, feeling paranoid as hell that this was the only place he'd take a call from his contact back in Miami. He didn't check in often, no names were exchanged, and each call required a new phone for that one call only. Still, having so much activity around the place made it next to impossible to control the environment. Even just having the name "Beulah, Alabama" in the national news was more attention than he liked.

"Of course they hide it well," Wynn snapped back at the guy on the other end of the line, a faceless voice, someone he didn't even know, someone he couldn't be certain he trusted with everything. With Annamae. "They don't do their own dirty work. They have too many legitimate income streams to risk playing a public role in their criminal activities."

"Except for the Antony Marks case," the other man observed dryly.

The murder Wynn witnessed. The one that would send Serge Dimitri to prison for life, assuming Wynn made it to the courthouse seventeen days from now. "An anomaly," Wynn dismissed. Serge was the family patriarch, but he hadn't been active in their dealings for years since he'd passed the business on to his son. "He's semi-retired ever since his oldest son took the reins from Serge a few years ago."

Wynn stared out the window at the rows of gnarled fruit trees probably better suited for burning than farming. But there was something peaceful out here in the sea of white blossoms, something that not even talk of the Dimitris could taint.

"Speaking of the younger generation," his contact said as he no doubt sat in a cool air-conditioned room, "you asked me to look for connections between that reality show actress—Annamae Jessup—and the Dimitri family."

"And?" He stilled, his hand gripping the phone tighter. He'd messaged that request on a secure server the day Annamae showed up at his gate.

"It's a small thing, but we did get a hit." The guy lowered his voice even though there was no sound in the background.

The idea didn't make sense. Annamae couldn't have a tie to the Dimitri family. Had someone followed her to town? Maybe the connection meant she was more at risk than he realized.

"What?" he prodded, edgy and pissed off. "What is it?"

"She placed a call to a radio talk show shortly before she drove to Beulah. Right on live radio, she broke up with that third baseman on the Stars—Boone Sullivan. The press is calling her the Hit and Run Bride."

A stab of jealousy went through him over her recent boy-friend and what now appeared to be her rebound escapades in Wynn's bed. Great. Just damn great. He should have thought to talk about that more before things had moved too fast and too well – too good – to be true. Living out here was taking away his edge.

He forced his mind back on the job, sorting through what his contact had said, sifting through the words for nuances and implications. A strange stab went through him, a possible betrayal so deep.... "Do the Dimitris own the radio station or something?"

They had their hand in the entertainment industry for sure. Hell, what if they even owned the network where her show aired? He'd briefly considered that possibility when he'd first met her, before she'd scrambled his brains.

"No. The woman Annamae called—the host of Sex Talk with Serena—is using a fake name." His connection rattled off facts like a well-versed expert on the Dimitri Crime Syndicate. "She's kept her identity a secret, but Serena is actually Valerie Dimitri. She's Serge's granddaughter."

"Hold on." He recalled Serge had many kids, most of them illegitimate. But the name Valerie didn't ring a bell. "Here is all I need to know. Is there any suggestion that Annamae contacted the Dimitri woman at any other time beyond the radio show?"

He saw a movement in the trees and reached for his

weapon, but then Bagel raced out of the trees, barking at some falling petals. A few seconds later, Annamae followed, her floral sundress rippling in the spring breeze.

"No. There's just that one call and it seems like all the rest of the Jessup girl's life is well documented."

That would be an understatement from what Annamae had described. He watched her now as she peered up into the branches of an apple tree, then moved to the ends of a low hanging limb to study the blossoms, arching up on her toes in sandals.

"I'll keep an eye on her," he assured his contact. "I'll check in next week and we can firm up plans for my relocation."

"Affirmative."

Disconnecting the call, Wynn opened his truck door. When he shut it, Bagel noticed him and came running. Annamae was slower to acknowledge his presence, but she did spin toward him, the sunlight making hints of caramel tones shimmer in her hair. She started walking toward him.

Not for a second did he believe she had any kind of connection to the Dimitri family, but he didn't like thinking that she'd come so close to one of them. He'd never heard of Valerie Dimitri, but that didn't mean she was clean. Serge liked to keep his family close. Most of the relatives were high visibility thugs.

"Hey." Fanning a slow wave, Annamae greeted him, far more subdued than her dog, who seemed to have developed a fair amount of affection for him. "I didn't expect to see you here."

Bagel raced to meet him, circling around his boots twice before trotting in step alongside.

"I checked the fences and then called in for an update." Slinging an arm around her shoulder, he pulled her to him, tucking her against his side. He didn't plan to tell her about the Dimitri connection. It wouldn't help her sleep any better at night and besides—he was watching over her now.

And the fact that she'd run from her own wedding? He needed to remember that the next time he got the urge to kiss her senseless. He should keep things simple. "What are you two doing out here?"

"I'm trying to recover from the talk with Mom." She twirled an apple blossom between her fingers. "Bagel is just along for the ride."

"I saw you really giving the trees a once-over." He was in no hurry to talk about anything of substance. No matter what he thought about the ex-fiancé, he still would have rather spent this day just messing around with her in his bed and maybe feeding each other strawberries.

She glanced up at him, her eyes as guarded as his own. "I read your book on grafting trees last night. You know you have a lot of old varieties on this land?"

He had to smile at that, their feet sinking in the soft spring earth.

"Is that so?" He knew, of course. Had been making elaborate schematics of the trees to identify them all.

Hiding out from crime families came with far too much downtime. Then again, farming had grown on him.

"Yes." She held up the blossom. "You have a lot of southern heirloom apples that can't be found anywhere else."

That he did *not* know.

"I should probably be taking better care of them then." Which meant he would have to stay here longer term, something he hadn't thought about. He liked this place.

"Yes, you should, if you want to stay and make any money." Annamae guided him toward one of the trees and pointed to the flowers, comparing a few of the blossoms to show him the differences.

"So I've got a mish mosh of varieties here and every other tree is going to yield up something weird and different?"

"Different isn't weird," she countered, before looking away. "My guess is the previous owner was a kind of collector of varieties. I'll bet the community garden would love to get some cuttings from these trees."

He watched her examine another branch of flowers while the breeze rained white petals on her hair. If he didn't have the trial coming up, he'd seriously consider kidnapping her for a year or two and seeing what happened between them.

Except that she'd just broken some other guy's heart five minutes before she rolled into town. Why the hell hadn't he paid more attention to what people said about the show or Googled it more extensively? He'd assumed the engagement was staged or some media lightweight affair. Now, feeling the deep emotions running through her, knowing her better, he wondered.

"You know all about cuttings after reading a chapter in a book?"

"More than a chapter. You took a long time to come to bed last night." She grinned at him over her shoulder, her eyes flirtatious, but still a hint of something sad lurked there. "I read a lot."

If there were any justice in the world, he'd be hauling her back to bed with him right now to kiss away that sadness, instead of playing host to her mother and worrying about how to keep them both safe.

"Well you made more sense of grafting than me. It sounds like I can't cut anything until the fall." When he'd be back in Miami and some other would-be farmer would benefit from all his hard work this year.

"Right. You wait until after they bear fruit. Then you need to take cuttings of them all this year so you can plant a fresh crop in the spring." She bit her lip, turning it apple red. "That is. If you decide to keep the land. Afterward."

And wasn't that the question of the decade for him? He had no idea what the future held for him, but his life was always going to be too dangerous for a woman like Annamae, a woman who lived in the limelight. And since he didn't want to think about a time without her, he steered them back to the present.

"So how did your mom find you? Did you ask why she decided to show up now to protest the broken engagement?" He fit her subtle curves to his side, inhaling the scent of her shampoo.

Bagel spotted a rabbit, but gave it the same greeting he offered to Wynn's cats—enthusiastic barking and panting.

Annamae whistled for her excitable pet and he found some enticing smelling leaves nearby.

"She has web alerts for whenever the Jessup name pops online. She saw the sighting and knew I might be in town because of Gram." She shrugged. "Anyway, Mom's just trying to get me to salvage something out of the mess I made back home. She'll want to spin it into a new reality episode about how she's helping me pick up the pieces of my shattered life." Sighing, she shrugged her shoulders. "I'm not certain my mother can separate life from the show anymore."

"Then send her on her way." He hardly dared to hope it would be that easy.

They kept walking through paths he'd followed hundreds of times in his year of Alabama solitude. It was a whole lot more fun with her at his side. Especially since she seemed to take so much pleasure out of the place. It was the second time he'd caught her unaware out walking, and he couldn't help but think she must like it here.

"She said something about my grandmother, about more secrets. And my grandmother has shared things about my mom that make it tougher to cut her off. I need to know.

More than that, I need to understand." She paused. "I'm like a poorly grafted apple tree." She grinned at her metaphor. "It's like I got glued on the wrong branch and I haven't thrived ever since."

"This is all about the Smith side of your family?" he clarified.

"Yes. My real father. And his mother."

He let that sink in, wishing there was another way for her to thrive without exposing her to more people and more time away from the security of the farm.

"Do you have to do this right now?"

"I believe I do, yes. For the first time in my life, I've grown a backbone. Do you realize how liberating that feels? Maybe not. You don't look like you've ever had trouble standing up for yourself." She looked him up and down, her eyes lingering in ways that made him contemplate a quickie in the back of his truck.

"I think that's a compliment," he said, hauling her closer, cupping her hips in his hands. "But it's not reassuring me. Don't mistake a backbone for recklessness."

Damn but he wanted her again. Now.

Last night hadn't come close to filling his hunger for her.

She looked up at him through long lashes that didn't need all the makeup she wore for her show. "Will my leaving here put you in danger?"

The concern in her voice slid right past his defenses, making him feel things for her that he definitely didn't want to be feeling. Steeling himself, he released her so they could keep on walking.

"Not unless you talked to your mother about who I am."

"Of course not. I just want to take her to the nursing home to see my grandmother so we can solve some family business. She doesn't even need to see you again, so there's no problem." She climbed up on an old tree root, balancing on a narrow, fallen tree for as long as she could until she teetered.

He caught her, taking his time for a thorough feel of her before he set her on her feet. Her cheeks were pink, he noticed.

"See, there we disagree," he said finally, wishing things were as simple as she'd tried to make them. "I worry that I am the one putting you in danger, which means I can't let you go to that nursing home again unescorted."

She kicked at a rotted part of the fallen log with the toe of her suede boot.

"If you escort me though, that means you'd have to leave the apple farm." That concern wove through her words again, and he knew he needed to stop liking that so damn much.

For her, he'd take a calculated risk.

"Have you already forgotten?" He traced a long line down her spine through the thin sweater she wore. "You're not the only one with a backbone."

Chapter Eight

"ANNAMAE? DID YOU plant flowers outside the carriage house?"

Wynn stopped the pickup truck in front of her new, temporary home. She followed his gaze to the window boxes she'd nailed together out of some boards she'd found in one of the old barns. And she'd done it with no one watching. Satisfying.

Fun.

"Aren't they great?" She admired the view of the carriage house while Bagel bounded out of the passenger side door to circle a favored tree. "Those wildflowers are growing like mad around an old fountain in back so I figured I'd transplant some. I know they'll probably wilt soon from the trauma of moving, but I'm sure they'll come back."

"Have I mentioned your DIY streak is really hot?" He kissed her neck and she forgot that she was supposed to be getting out of the truck.

Closing her eyes, she enjoyed the moment and the man. How delicious was it to do something because you wanted to and not because you were supposed to? Here, she could linger. She wasn't on a schedule. Here, she could run out without makeup and no one cared. Wynn thought she was sexy from her dark blonde roots to her do-it-yourself efforts around the farm.

"You're going to make it difficult for me to leave," she murmured, shivering when he did something erotic with his tongue just beneath her ear.

"You're not allowed to leave." His mouth worked lower, nudging aside her sweater along her collarbone. "This is going to be a Beauty and the Beast thing where I hold you captive in my private lair and keep you all to myself." He paused his kissing trek. "Unless you're having second thoughts about breaking up with that ex-fiancé of yours?"

Had he been worrying about that? She ducked to look into his eyes and realized, yes, he had. At least a little. They hadn't talked about Boone much at all, which should have said damn plenty, considering she'd been naked with this man last night.

She stroked both sides of his face, the stubble deliciously bristly against her palms as their gazes met. "I can assure you, one hundred percent, I am not having second thoughts about breaking up with Boone. There may be a lot of things I'm confused about in my life. But that decision? I'm dead certain it was the right one."

"Okay, then." He tipped his head to resume nuzzling her neck.

Her sweater was already sliding off her shoulder, exposing her tank top and a bra strap. He slipped his finger beneath both straps and tugged them down.

Desire sparked. Flamed. She debated stretching out on the bench seat of his old pickup right now.

"You forget my mom is inside that house, waiting for me." She wasn't crazy about the idea either, but there it was.

Slowly, he straightened. Kissed her shoulder and reassembled her clothes. "I'll come back and kidnap you when she's sleeping tonight."

"Or I can just sneak out." She wanted another night in his arms. Another week or ten.

"I'm counting on it. If you're not in my bed at midnight, Cinderella, I'm coming to get you."

"You're mixing up your fairytales." She kissed his bristly jaw. His cheek.

"You're my first fairytale kind of girl." He shrugged. "Give a guy a break."

"In that case, you just go right on mixing it up." She was already regretting not getting naked on the front seat with him. But she edged back, buying herself a little breathing room to collect herself. "I'll see you before tonight though if you're going to the retirement center with us?"

"What time?" He checked his watch.

"Six?" She pulled a folded brochure out from her purse. "I picked up a bunch of literature that day I went to see her before and this was in there."

She pointed to the ad for a hoedown dance tonight—a

mixer with the residents from another retirement center from the next town over.

"We're going to a hoedown?" He scratched his head.

"I've only met Hazel Mae twice and I already know she'll be there. I have a good feeling my grandmother wouldn't miss a hoedown."

Wynn squeezed his temples. "I hope we can get her outside."

"Of course. But I'll go incognito, just in case."

"Really?" He brightened, liking that idea, apparently.

"I make a sexy brunette," she promised. "Especially in jean shorts."

"You'll incite heart attacks in record numbers, Red. Not a good idea."

"I'm teasing." She slid across the seat and levered the door open wider. "About the jean shorts anyway. See you tonight."

"THIS IS UTTERLY ridiculous, Annamae."

Her mother glared at her as they walked underneath an arch made of hay and threaded with daisies. Red bandanas served as centerpieces on every table in the facility's transformed auditorium. A country music tribute band played tunes from the late, great Lara Kane while a few couples two-stepped around the dance floor.

"I think it's adorable," she whispered back, accepting a plastic cup of lemonade from a server dressed in a leather fringe skirt and plaid western blouse. "I hope I'm still dancing in my advanced years."

"I don't mean them," her mother grumbled. "I mean us."

Annamae hid a snicker, knowing perfectly well why her mother was miffed. She hadn't been out of the house in an outfit that wasn't approved by her stylist in a decade.

"You refused to change your hair color, so you had to have the cowgirl hat. End of discussion." Annamae had resurrected her red scarf from her bargain store shopping spree on her way into Alabama. She'd given her mother a chambray shirt she'd bought that day too, but her mother was more upset about her homemade skirt.

"Burlap and recycled lace curtains do not add up to clothing in any universe," her mother shot back. "I'm actually grateful for the white straw atrocity on my head to ensure no one sees my face in this sack you call a skirt."

"Scarlett O'Hara wore curtains, mom. Embrace your southern side." Annamae passed a window on the exterior wall of the room and peered out to look for signs of Wynn. He'd driven them to the retirement center and walked them into the party, but promptly disappeared to take a look around outside.

As much as she'd like to wish he were paranoid, his constant vigilance made her wary. She didn't like doing things that could draw attention to him or his farm so no matter how much her mother groused, they were remaining incognito tonight.

"Besides," she continued. "At least this way I can be sure you're not secretly filming footage to send home." Annamae searched the crowd for a Hazel Mae sighting but didn't see her grandmother. "I know you'd never appear on television that way, although I think you look great."

The musicians changed the tempo. Slowing things down with an old Patsy Cline song. As the party quieted, a loud laugh caught her attention. And her mother's too. Their heads turned as one to see Annamae's grandmother stride through the hay and daisy arch with a younger man on her arm.

"Will you look at her?" Delilah shook her head and sipped her lemonade. "You should thank your lucky stars you got her genes. I've never seen such good skin on a woman older than me. Although why she always insisted on that horrid color for her hair—."

"Mom." Annamae turned on her. "Stop it. You are not on camera. No one wants to hear catty comments. In the real world, it's not entertaining. It's just mean."

She kept her voice pitched low, but she couldn't take any more *Acting Up* behavior in Beulah.

Her mother's eyes narrowed as if she debated going in for round two. But she took another sip of her lemonade and said, "Fine. Just fine. Let's go get this family party over with, okay?"

As concessions went, it was practically graceful.

Not wanting to push her luck, Annamae headed through the crowd toward her grandmother and hoped that she could pull her away from the party discreetly.

"Hazel Mae," she said softly just behind her grandmother's ear.

Making the older woman jump.

"You scared me, young lady!" Hazel Mae looked ready to start a scene, her hand clutching her chest, when she seemed to recognize Annamae. "Er—watch yourself, dear. You should go check out the laser light show outside. If you go early you'll get a good seat."

Annamae nodded. Her grandmother could have a second career working undercover. For all Annamae knew, Hazel Mae might have. She was still a mystery. And probably a far better actress than her.

Heading back toward her mother, Annamae linked her arm through hers and explained their destination. For a moment, the gesture of walking with her mother minus the cameras, felt normal. As if this was what it was like to be mother and daughter. As if this was what she had been missing for years. Family sans cameras. "We're meeting outside. I'll get your sweater."

Sidling out of the hoedown through a side door, Annamae almost ran into Wynn stalking along the wide porch in his black Stetson and an old leather duster. He looked like he'd just stepped off a Western film set. Or like he'd finished a set on stage for a country music show. Even in disguise, he was hot.

"Excuse me," Annamae mumbled as she brushed past him, knowing better than to speak to him. He'd schooled her on how things would go this evening before they left the house. He was driving them. He was looking out for them.

But they were to have as little contact as possible.

Annamae averted her eyes and kept walking with her mother. She forced the memory of last night—and the promise of tonight—out of her mind. It was time to focus on family. She'd deal with her feelings for Wynn later.

Her mother harrumphed under her breath, but Annamae, in turn, had schooled her mom on the etiquette required for staying in Beulah. No antics. No cameras. No revealing their identities at anytime, to anyone.

It didn't matter that the town knew Annamae had been there. As far as anyone else was aware, she'd already left. And it needed to stay that way for her sake. For Wynn's safety.

She swallowed hard as she led her mom out onto the back lawn where chairs were set up for the light show. They were empty except for one amorous-looking couple off the side. Annamae was debating where to sit when Hazel Mae exited the building from another door and stalked off toward the garden.

Perfect.

"This way." She led her mother past the water-spouting

angels. Only a few trees were lit at night, leaving most of the garden in darkness. She took a different path than her grandmother, but she had the feeling she knew where they'd both end up.

Right where they'd spoken last time.

"Hell's bells, girl. What did you bring her here for?" Grandma's voice lifted as she recognized Delilah.

Shushing her, Annamae backed the group toward a brick bench around a small water fountain.

"Bet you hoped you'd never have to see me again, didn't you, Hazel?" Delilah taunted.

"Not in that get-up, that's for sure." Hazel flicked a glance over the burlap skirt. "What in tarnation are you wearing?"

"Oh don't go all hillbilly on me, Hazel. Is this how you charmed my daughter, by pretending to be a harmless little redneck from backwoods Alabama?" She fluttered her lashes in an affectation of innocence.

"We are not creating a scene," Annamae announced. "I mean it. I'm here for answers and I'm not interested in posturing, so both of you can either get on board with being forthright or we're done here."

Night birds chirped in the silence that followed. Sounds of steel guitars and fiddles drifted on the cool air.

"I am ready to be civil," her grandmother announced.

"This is your show, honey," her mother managed through gritted teeth.

"Excellent." Annamae thought she felt her backbone stiffen. She was actually making headway here. "Grandma, meeting was Mom's idea. She hoped we could get everything out in the open so—."

"Halleluiah." Hazel Mae lifted her hands to the heavens. "So she told you how I tried to get custody of you? That's how much I wanted you in my life, sweetheart. I tried. But who could fight with the kinds of lawyers her rich sugar daddy could afford?"

Annamae slumped back on the brick bench. Had she thought she'd grown a backbone? The news seeped all the newfound steel right out of her. Why had her mother lied and lied to her?

"What kind of grandmother tries to steal a mother's birth right?" Delilah was saying.

Only with more venom.

Annamae realized she'd need a dedicated referee to get to the bottom of this. And having this conversation here wasn't a good idea. Anyone could pass by the garden without being seen, the foliage thick and the night dark.

"Grandma?" she interrupted the quarrel, feeling far too weary for seven p.m. "Would you mind coming to stay with us for a day or two so we can have this discussion without worrying about... er... prying eyes?"

Both the other women looked over their shoulders, the gestures so alike they could have been the ones who were related.

"Of course, sweetie." Hazel Mae stood. "I'm a resident here by choice, not because I'm on my death bed. I'll just call and let them know I won't be home tonight."

"Heaven help us." Delilah swigged her lemonade down so fast Annamae would have sworn it must be spiked, but she'd had a glass too, and it was just the tasty, homemade real thing.

"Come on." Annamae gestured toward the parking lot. "Let's get out of here and we'll figure this out at home."

Home?

When had Wynn's place become so dear to her? More emotions to sort out later.

Darting across the dew-damp lawn with her mother and grandmother—dressed in burlap and bandanas—Annamae had to laugh. She'd been in the carriage house for just a few days, but that's exactly how it felt—like where she belonged.

All those years she'd wanted to be a part of a perfect family portrait and hadn't quite fit. Yet right now, with two feuding women at her side and stealing through the night like thieves, she felt more a part of a family than she ever had before.

THE JESSUP PRESENCE in Beulah was growing every day.

Wynn fumed silently as he drove Annamae and company back to the farm. He should have never opened that gate to her the first time. Every minute spent off his land was a risk to his safety, to the trial. Every new person who set foot on his property was a risk. Knowing Annamae had forced him to take too many chances.

With himself. With her. With a case that meant too much to him to screw up now.

They needed to talk tonight. Get everyone out of town—preferably out of the state of Alabama—and out of his life before his whereabouts was exposed.

Now, he checked the rearview mirror again, and saw the same pair of headlights that had been behind him earlier. Even though he'd taken a few convoluted turns that took them farther from the farm.

No doubt about it, the truck was being followed while he had three generations of women in cowboy gear and not a gun to be had between them. How had he let himself ignore his instincts? He should have kept the women at his place.

For seventeen days?

"We're being followed," he announced in his best controlled voice, the one he used to talk jumpers away from the ledge. He had training. Now was the time to use it.

A slightly tipsy Delilah swatted his shoulder from the back seat. "Don't be silly. No one lives out here and you took the back road."

"Precisely my point, ma'am." He pointed to the rearview mirror, headlights glowing behind them.

"Oh," Delilah stretched up until her face popped up into

the mirror's reflection too.

Hazel Mae hissed, grabbing her seatmate by the neck scarf. "If we're being followed, don't block his view with your hundred dollar hairdo."

"I did my hair myself this morning, I'll have you know."

"Well, goodie for you. Glad to know your six weeks in cosmetology school taught you something."

"Mom?" Annamae had been quiet up until now. "You went to beauty school?"

"I did not," Delilah insisted.

"Liar," Hazel retorted.

Annamae shook her head. "I can't believe the press missed that detail."

"Ladies," Wynn interrupted, taking a quick turn that slid them all sideways in their seats. "If y'all want to keep talking, could you at least duck down where I don't have to worry about some crime lord or drunk redneck shooting the back of your head off?"

All three women hit the floorboards.

Annamae peered up at him, the dashboard glow reflecting off her face. "You don't have to be that graphic. You could scare my grandmother into a heart attack."

Delilah harrumphed. "We should be so lucky."

Hazel waved over the seat. "No worries, granddaughter dear. I'm just fine. Having the time of my life actually. Anyone else hoping for a hot renegade like one of those sexy *Sons of Anarchy*?"

"Ha," Delilah answered, "your wish isn't going to come true tonight. Because unless I miss my guess, the lights on that car belong to a man who's only going to be out to shoot me and my daughter."

Wynn's eyes narrowed as he yanked the steering wheel into a hard turn. "Care to enlighten me?"

"From what little you let me see in the rearview mirror, I am almost certain that's my husband following us."

Wynn noted the shape of the headlights as the sports car sped up. The distinctive nose and the glint of a hood ornament appeared right before the Georgia State vanity plate came into view.

JESSUP1

Holy hell.

"So much for keeping a low profile." He hadn't asked his contact back in Miami to investigate the whole Jessup family, but now he wished he had. This guy was the TV producer.

The Dimitri family had entertainment world connections. That was a fact. If the media were here. Well, he was in more danger than he could imagine. Danger he had practically invited in.

"He must be worried about Mom." Annamae adjusted her mirror. "Can we talk to him back at the farm?"

Wynn didn't think forcing Jessup off the road and into a ditch was an option, but he took his time contemplating it anyhow.

And ended up circling back toward the farm.

"I am not comfortable having all these people on property I'm trying to keep secure." He needed to get rid of everyone but Annamae.

Although a smarter man would have sent her packing too.

"Would you have rather we had this discussion on the side of the road? Because once he started tailgating us, there really wasn't any other option but to bring him with us." Annamae twisted a leather bracelet around and around her thin wrist.

"Anyone else in the family you want to invite in before I put this place on lockdown?" he asked, a knife-edge in his voice. He slowed as he approached the gate, reaching for his remote and thumbing in security clearance codes.

From the jump seat, Hazel Mae leaned forward, her eyes on the fence swinging open electronically.

"You turned the old Hastings place into Fort Knox!" She clapped Wynn on the shoulder. "You might not know it, but this place hasn't had prize-winning apples in a long time, young man. There's not much worth locking up back here anymore."

"Matter of opinion, ma'am." Wynn tried not to glare at her as he drove through and let Annamae's stepfather do the same.

"You're mad and I understand," Annamae said softly

once her grandmother leaned back in her seat. "I'm so sorry."

"Damn it, Annamae, don't go all reasonable on me and deflate a solid pissed off moment."

"I need to talk to my father, but after that, maybe I can convince him to take Mom back home." She slid off the red bandana she'd worn for the hoedown.

His eyes went to her profile, hungry for a glimpse of her even though he had every right to be angry about how this night had turned out.

"You might as well bring them to the big house." He wanted her in his sight at all times and he hadn't appreciated how aggressively her stepfather drove when he knew his wife and Annamae were in the other vehicle. He'd be keeping an eye on the guy. "You'll never fit all of them in the carriage house."

"Thank you." Her eyes found his in the dim interior as he pulled to a stop. "I'll try to wrap things up fast—before my mom and my grandmother eat each other alive."

Already, her mother was bolting out of the truck and calling to her husband. Hazel Mae followed more slowly, grumbling about "self-aggrandizing pompous asses."

"You promised to see me tonight," Wynn reminded Annamae, even though he'd been wrestling with the idea of her ex-fiancé for the better part of the day.

He wasn't cut out for the convoluted family dynamics, the over-the-top behavior or the superficial lives the Jessups led. And while he saw something different in Annamae, he also couldn't deny the running away from her celebrity wedding was exactly the kind of reality TV stunt that he didn't need in his life.

His world was dangerous. And undercover. Or at least, it had been until the Jessups descended on it.

She kissed his cheek before she slid out of the truck. "That's a promise I can keep."

Making him wonder how many others she wouldn't.

Chapter Nine

H AD SHE ENDANGERED Wynn?
The fear niggled while she stood outside the farmhouse living room listening to her stepfather rattle on about how far he would go to protect the Jessup family empire.

As if sportswear was such a crucial commodity?

Tuning him out long enough to collect her thoughts, Annamae still didn't enter the room, hiding in the shadows as if she was back in the family mansion in Buckhead. It was back to beige, back to her role as the dutiful spineless daughter, she supposed.

The thought gnawed at her stomach almost as consistently as blowing Wynn's cover. She took a deep breath. Then another. This didn't have to be her story. Somewhere, deep down, she knew that.

By now, she was used to disappointing Spencer Jessup III. But she wasn't used to being so thoroughly disappointed by him. The reality show may give his brand visibility and be great for sales, but what about what was good for Annamae?

Sure, he had no way of knowing that he endangered

Wynn and everyone else on the farm by showing up in Beulah. But he did know that she wanted privacy and some time out of the spotlight. She'd texted her family the request on her way out of Atlanta. At least her mother had attempted to keep a low profile. Her stepfather, on the other hand, drove a flashy sports car with his name on the plates, assuring he'd be noticed. This was just the kind of publicity to spike *Acting Up*'s ratings. The runaway bride dragged back home from a reprieve in the countryside. This kind of drama could ensure national syndication.

If his need for publicity cost Wynn his case—or worse— she'd be handing the Jessup name back to him.

With a sigh, she turned on her heel and entered the room. Even though there was no camera rolling, it struck her how her parents staged themselves without even receiving direction. Years of constant cameras meant the Jessups naturally arranged themselves in the most dramatic shots.

Delilah's posture was perfect as she sat on a padded Queen Anne chair on one side of the room. Spencer stood to her right, one hand on her shoulder. They looked like they were shooting a promotional video for the next season. Annamae's mind whirred. This is why she needed space. To figure out what reality actually looked like.

On the opposite side of the sparsely furnished area, Hazel Mae had claimed the faded floral couch for herself.

"Annamae, I hope you've packed your things. You can ride home with your mother and me." He checked his phone, scrolling through messages. Her stepfather was only half-present it seemed, bound to the device in his hand.

She winced, knowing how much Wynn discouraged phones' location features.

"Dad." She cleared her throat. "I would appreciate it if you'd either turn off the cell or at least disable the location setting. I've worked hard to let the public think I've left Alabama."

Not to mention, Wynn's safety depends on that continued belief.

As well-dressed as his wife normally would be, Spencer Jessup could have been in one of his advertisements. His brand thrived in better department stores—high end, but attainable—and he repped it at all times. This year's nautical motif came through in the navy cloth belt that he wore with his khakis, his pressed white button-down made more casual with a red and white sweater vest. His boat shoes probably cost more than her VW Beetle.

He stared at her blankly. "And you *will* be out of Alabama. Within the hour. So I'm sure it doesn't matter. Would you like help with your bags?"

She grit her teeth, wondering who he'd call to help with the bags if she said yes. Certainly, he had no plans to carry anything himself. That wasn't his style.

"Pfft." Her grandmother made a rude sound, shaking her head. "His mama forgot to teach him he's not the only person on the planet. Want me to take his phone from him, darlin'?"

Annamae shook her head, wondering if she'd dreamed that foolish moment of camaraderie with her mother and grandmother.

"Don't be silly, Hazel." Delilah slid the phone from her husband's fingers and tucked it in her purse. "He was just finishing an important business meeting."

Spencer scowled, but didn't argue. Hazel Mae rolled her eyes.

"Dad, why are you even here?" Annamae took a seat beside her grandmother on the old couch beside a player piano. One of Wynn's more sluggish looking felines lay across the closed roll top, swishing its tail, eyeing the scene with intense feline disinterest.

The black and white kitten who'd been on her bed the night before sat on the piano bench, watching the other cat's tail go back and forth like a metronome, probably timing a pounce.

"To support you, of course." He spoke his lines like an old-time soap opera star, with a bit too much drama.

Then again, maybe her thoughts were as catty and judgmental as she accused her mother of being.

"I appreciate the thought." She reminded herself to be fair. "But I had asked you and Mom to give me some space to figure this out."

"Yes, but we knew the kind of…" he said, eyes going to Hazel "*influences* that awaited you here. And I'm not about to let that woman tear apart my family."

"This ought to be good." Hazel Mae leaned forward. "Do tell, Spence. Are you afraid Annamae might learn the truth about how much we wanted to keep her away from you? Too late. She already knows."

"Oh for crying out loud, Hazel." Delilah jumped to her feet, clearly agitated. "It's not that. He doesn't want you and Earl showing up on the set of the show and turning it into some hillbilly joke."

Silence settled, the heavy, embarrassed kind of quiet. And she knew right then, she wasn't as catty as her mother because that hadn't crossed her mind.

Hazel picked at her bracelets, mumbling, "Apparently money doesn't buy manners."

Annamae agreed one hundred percent. Then another thought hit her. "Is my father even on this continent?" Annamae demanded, trying to get a read on all their expressions. She watched Hazel Mae exchange a glance with Delilah.

"I thought he was in Australia. Or was that some made up story?"

That her grandmother would have lied and her mother would have gone along? That stung.

Hazel looked up, jaw jutting. "Believe what you want. Time for you to start making your own assessments without a crew deciding for you."

Ouch.

Thank God her father rose, all full of drama, saving her from answering that too astute comment.

"Delilah, I came here to bring you home." He picked up her mother's purse and handed it to her. "Annamae, dear, we want you to leave with us. This woman has never had your best interests at heart."

Annamae didn't know whom to trust. No one looked at her square in the eye except for—oddly—her stepfather.

"I'd like to be the judge of that," she told him flatly. "I need some more time to think things over, but I appreciate you caring enough to come all the way here and talk to me."

"Come back to Atlanta with us," her mother urged, placing a well-lotioned hand over hers. "We don't have to talk about this now, or the broken engagement on the show—."

"No." She shook her head, snatching her hand away, unwilling to justify her actions to a woman who didn't listen to her anyway. Any accord they'd shared earlier seemed to have faded when her stepfather showed up. Was this the price of security over wild love? Was this what life would have looked like had she decided to stay with Boone?

Would her mother have been a much different person if she'd married Earl Smith? A woman Annamae might have really related to? But at least she understood her mom better. Understood that her mother had the capacity for an un-scripted adventure, even if she stifled those urges now.

And Annamae was on the way to understanding more about herself, oddly enough in the way Wynn just ...

accepted her. No lights and script. Just Annamae. Plain and simple.

"That's just the thing, Mom. I can't sweep this under the rug. I need to face what I've done, but I'm going to gather my strength here first. I'll go back when I'm ready." She squeezed her mother's hand, face earnest. Delilah nodded slightly, eyes warming to the truth in her daughter's words. Maybe she was wrong to have second-guessed her mother's camaraderie earlier.

Spencer patted her on the shoulder before heading for the door. "The script writers will come up with something, sweetheart. Don't worry."

Delilah followed him. "I need to change first, Spence. You don't want to be around me dressed like this." Once he left the room, she hugged Annamae. "I'll make sure we keep the lid on Beulah. You try to do the same here, okay? We don't want to advertise the Alabama connection any more than you do."

"Thank you, Mom." She stepped over a big orange tabby cat snoozing in the middle of a big braid rug. "I appreciate you respecting my privacy."

"Be careful with the apple farmer and all his cats," Delilah warned. "Any man with that many locks on his doors has secrets to hide."

A comment too astute by half. Her mother saw too much. She needed to leave.

"Seems to me we all have our secrets to keep under lock

and key, missy," Hazel Mae piped up, coming slowly to her feet.

For the first time since Annamae met her, her grandmother looked her age. No doubt she was tired from all the drama. Annamae felt more than a little weary too.

She wanted nothing so much as to find Wynn and lose herself in his arms.

"Your grandmother has a soft spot in her heart for reprobates," Delilah warned. "Just ask her."

Without another word she turned on her heel and marched out of the room in her burlap skirt.

Hazel Mae chuckled softly. "She thinks she's so damn different from my son but honey, if you met your daddy, you'd see they were a match in every way. She runs right over that Spencer fellow like he's a nautical colored rug."

Annamae didn't think that was entirely accurate, but she could see her grandmother's point. Relationships were ... complicated. More than she'd realized before she'd even dialed up the Sex Talk lady. Which didn't give her a lot of confidence for how she would handle things with Wynn and wherever their affair was going.

They were having an affair, right? It wasn't a one night stand. And she wasn't her mom, so unsure of what she wanted out of life that she hopped from one guy to the next, leaving a trail of wreckage behind.

She would take things one day at a time. He had too much uncertainty in his future. He didn't need pressure and confusion from her. And yet, her heart squeezed in panic over ... making a bad decision or making a good decision because either way she didn't get to stay in limbo.

Hazel patted her cheek. "Quit thinking so hard."

Now why hadn't she thought of that?

"You're right. Let's just enjoy this evening. Tomorrow, I'm going to quiz you all about my dad," she informed her, taking her by the arm. "I've got a lot of questions. But first, I'm going to let you rest. You're going to love my carriage house."

And once she had her grandmother snoozing through her night away from the retirement home, Annamae intended to take her grandmother's advice about living in the moment. For tonight at least.

WYNN PROMISED TO have Delilah Jessup's BMW returned to Atlanta at his earliest convenience, knowing damn well it wouldn't be convenient until after that Dimitri trial. He'd personally escorted the Jag out the back entrance, pleased that Spencer hadn't notice the mud Wynn had caked on the license plate while the guy had been talking to Annamae.

It didn't do anything to make the car less flashy, but at least it didn't announce Annamae's family name in neon lights.

Now, he finished up in the barns for the night, making

sure the outdoor cats had some chow. The light had gone out in the carriage house half an hour ago. He hoped that meant Annamae would be waiting for him when he got in.

What a farce of a night it had been—a hoedown, a car chase, a trio of half-crazy relatives. The woman had turned his life upside down. If not for the risk to her and to the trial though, he wouldn't even care. He could tell himself all day long that her romantic history was a problem, and it probably didn't bode well for any kind of future even if his job and her fame didn't mix. Yet that didn't diminish the fact that being with her was the first hint of happiness he'd felt in a long time.

Inside the house, he took his time showering in the downstairs bathroom, needing to be sure she had enough time to get in his house and in his bed. He needed her to be there when he got out. Needed it with a hunger that verged on...

Hell. He just needed her.

Some things were that simple.

Drying off, he raked his fingers through his hair and wrapped a towel around his waist. He padded along the hardwood floors toward the stairs, shutting off lights and double checking locks as he went.

A red scarf trailed over the banister.

His heart kicked up speed. Everything else was kicking up too, taking the towel with it.

He charged up the rest of the steps. The door of his bedroom was shut, the barest hint of light emanating from beneath. Opening it, he found the bed empty. But the upstairs shower was running. Annamae's voice hummed a tune that drifted through the bathroom door.

Picturing her naked and wet made his brain shut off. She was just on the other side of that door. Ready for him.

All for him.

A surge of possessiveness surged through him, the need to eradicate the ex-boyfriend became a Neanderthal calling in his blood. Levering open the heavy exterior door, he saw her in the frame-less shower—a luxury he'd allowed himself when he moved in, and a gift that kept giving since it revealed Annamae swaying like a wood nymph under the overhead rainfall.

He dropped his towel and she peeked over one shoulder for an instant before he slid his arms around her waist and captured her from behind.

Her hair was dark on her back, slick with water. He buried his face in her neck, inhaling her scent and tasting her there. She smelled like his shampoo, his soap, but somehow, still like Annamae. With a soft sigh on her lips, she went limp in his arms.

She rolled her hips against him, rubbing herself against his twitching erection. He wanted to sink inside her—badly. And she made it damn obvious she was ready for him to. But he wanted to take his time. Burn away thoughts of everything but him.

Spinning her in his arms, he pressed her against the tile, watching the water run in rivulets over her lithe body. She watched him right back, her gaze curious. Hungry.

He licked a stream of water that ran down her neck, following the trail to her breast until he circled the taut peak. She reached for him, her fingers digging into his shoulders as he drew on her, giving equal attention to each beautiful breast. Then he followed another rivulet lower. Lower. He sank to his knees in front of her and her eyes went wide. He wrapped his hands around her thighs and she went boneless as he tasted the slick heat of her.

So wet. So ready. So his.

Her breath caught and held her hands moving over his back in restless circles. He moved deeper, working his mouth against her harder. She melted on his tongue.

Her release went through her in waves, each lush convulsion making her cry out. When he was sure he'd wrung every ounce of pleasure from her gorgeous body, he lifted her in his arms and shut off the shower. She clung to him, her lips murmuring sweet things in his ear while he juggled a towel awkwardly over them both. He wasn't even sure she noticed, her mouth moving to his neck. His lips.

She tasted like toothpaste.

He carried her to his bed and tossed her in the center amid sheets still tangled from where they'd left off that morning. He had a sudden urge to see her there every morning. Every night. But he didn't let himself think about that. Not now. Not when they still had this window of time together.

"I hope you're going to join me." She peered up at him through her lashes, her whole body flushed pink from the hot water and pleasure.

"I'm trying to figure out how many ways I can have you before dawn." He could look at her all night long.

"Maybe you can do your calculations at the same time you're—." She gestured toward his body. "You know. Letting me feel you up."

"*You're* going to feel *me* up?" Laughing, he covered her, knowing damn well that he couldn't last long once his body started touching hers.

"Yes." She wriggled beneath him in a way that made his whole body pay attention.

And that was before her fingers slipped between them to stroke him from base to tip.

"See?" she breathed in his ear, flirty and sweet at the same time.

"I see." The words cracked in his suddenly dry throat. "But I get to do all the feeling up tonight."

He palmed her breast, lifting the soft weight of her and circling the sensitive spot that made her moan and open her thighs for him. Grappling along the nightstand for a condom with his other hand, he rolled it on and nudged his way inside her. Deep. Deeper.

She fit him like she was made for him alone. He gripped

her hips and sank into her over and over, burning with the need that had ridden him all day. She wrapped her legs around him. Locked her ankles. Held him where she wanted him.

When she came the next time, he hurtled with her, calling her name and holding onto her tight. The pleasure went on and on, the force of all he'd been holding back throttling through him now until he was wrung out and empty. He didn't let her go. Couldn't let her go.

For tonight, she was his Annamae. And he had sixteen more days to keep it that way.

THE NEXT MORNING, she stood in the farmhouse's quiet kitchen, fighting the urge not to cook breakfast.

In her fantasy life, that's exactly what she'd do. She would invite Bagel and his cat posse outside with her to enjoy the spring sunshine, then she'd pick around the old cottage garden that Wynn had partially resurrected with a few new plantings. With any luck, she'd find some fresh herbs and use them to season some eggs. Maybe make homemade biscuits so the whole place smelled like warm, baking things. The whole thing would be a scene of domestic bliss.

Then she'd wake Wynn and feed him the feast while she watched him eat. Regain his strength so he could take her back to his bed...

Pure fantasy.

She'd had her stolen hours with Wynn. She'd indulged in a blissful night of not thinking so hard. She knew it couldn't go on this way. Not when there was so much unresolved back home. Her parents' unorthodox family meeting had reminded her of that.

Sliding down to a seat at the scarred kitchen table, she pulled one of his disposable phones from the plastic package so she could check her voicemail. She'd have to pay him back with one of hers. For now though, she connected to her service and heard her best friend's voice.

"Hey Annamae, it's Lindsey." Her words came out in a rush, sounding nervous and not at all like Lindsey. "I know it's a hard week for you and I want to respect what you're going through. I do. But I'm kinda losing it here with my own wedding coming up and if there's any way on God's green earth we could hang out for a few hours before I have to say my own vows... Or even if I just knew you'd be there when I walked down the aisle..." She paused to sniff. "Call me, okay? Or just be here for the wedding."

Frowning, Annamae played the message again, almost not believing her unflappable friend was so distraught. Then again, Annamae knew how much a wedding could shake a girl up. Lindsey needed her.

Not because Annamae was a TV personality or because she was related to a rich, semi-famous family. Lindsey was a real friend who knew her. Annamae. Not the false façade.

And the real Annamae didn't want to be the kind of person who ran away from trouble. She wanted to be the kind of woman who solved them. She couldn't be like her father, stepfather, mother or even grandmother. She had to find herself.

In Atlanta.

Where her real life—her friends—waited. She'd been hiding out here, pretending to search for answers when she was really just making excuses for the drama her life had become. That's not the way grown-ups behaved. And she refused to play a role that was assigned to her anymore.

Getting to her feet, she left the used phone on the table along with a note for Wynn. She'd say goodbye before she left, of course. For now, she just let him know she would be back at the carriage house doing some packing.

Her fantasy time was over.

Chapter Ten

I T WAS BAD enough to wake up alone after nightmares about the shooting.

Wynn was used to that.

But waking up to the sound of Annamae loading the VW Beetle? It was just plain cruel. He could hear her shifting around boxes and calling out orders to her dog and grandmother. This was what he got after the night they'd shared?

He pulled on a pair of jeans and stomped down the stairs. The cats didn't even congregate to lend moral support. They were already outside with her, overseeing the proceedings as she tried to utilize every square inch of her backseat.

"Where the hell do you think you're going?" He stood between her and the car.

She bit her lip, face flushed red. Sorry she was going? Or sorry she'd gotten caught in the act?

"To Atlanta." She moved to go around him.

He took the box out of her hands and dropped it on top of a yellow gym bag with the price tags still attached.

"Back to your show?"

"No, back to pick up the wreckage I made of my life."
She swiped a stray hair from her cheek and tucked it behind
her ear. "I need to fix some things."

"Right." His lips thinned into a tight line.

"You don't believe me." She backed up a step, steadying
herself on the wrought iron railing alongside the carriage
house steps.

"Frankly? No. Why should I? I barely know you, but I
sure have seen the way you run on high drama. I hear your
show is thriving since you shot the runaway bride episode."

"Do you have to be cruel? Are you the only one who gets
to be a big badass grownup who does the right thing? I can't
keep hiding out here and just ignoring the parts of my life
that haven't worked out the way Mom does." She straightened some plants leaning sideways in the window box she'd
made, not looking at him. "I need to face the music before I
can move on with my life."

Bagel gave a bark, pacing around their feet.

"Moving on with your life? What does that even mean?
You haven't been living while you've been here?"

At that, she turned slowly.

"I've been hiding and I'm not going to do that anymore." She folded her arms. Stared him down.

"Right. You don't want to hide. You want to move on."
He stared at the window boxes full of wildflowers on the
carriage house behind her, trying to picture how he could
stay here without her. "Which I'm still not clear on. But the

point is, you're leaving. That much I get."

"I need to do the right thing. Then, I'll move back here and ..." she peered around the farm and her voice lost some steam. "I'll do ... something."

"You definitely sound ready to face the world." Knowing how little thought she'd given to her safety pissed him off. He'd need to have her watched, protected, until his trial was done.

But he wasn't about to let anything happen to her even though she was breaking their agreement. Had she ever intended to keep a low profile for more than five minutes?

"You're not being fair." She blinked fast, the hint of emotion almost getting to him.

And then he remembered she'd done this to some other poor sap just last week.

"Neither are you, Annamae. And I think you know it." Steel wedged in his voice.

Their silent standoff was broken when Hazel Mae stepped out of the carriage house, banging the screen door behind her.

"All set!" When she saw him, she smiled. "Morning, Mr. Lambert. And my, don't you look a sight without your shirt on." She fanned herself, winking at him. "Not fair to an old lady, that's for darn sure."

Annamae stepped away from him. Wynn knew he had to let her go.

"You're going to Atlanta too?" he managed, trying to be

polite even though his tone came out flat. Cold.

The older woman didn't seem to notice.

"Annamae's best friend is getting married, and as it happens, I do love a wedding."

"Let's hope she has better luck tying the knot than Annamae." He stared directly at Annamae, trying to force her to look at him. A tightness in his chest pulsed.

Hazel rattled on about weddings and how Annamae had been smart to recognize that she hadn't been engaged to the right man.

Annamae remained silent. A shade paler than she'd been a minute ago. The woman he'd spent the best night of his life with didn't have one damn thing to say to him. He'd hurt her.

Guess that made two of them.

"Ready, Gram?" Annamae called across the car as she scooped up her dog.

"I was born ready, honey. You take after me, you know." Hazel Mae winked at him.

Annamae edged around him and opened the driver's side door of her car.

"I *will* be back. Whether you want to see me or not." She tied her scarf around her hair.

"And you know damn well I won't be here if you do." He held her door for her while she got in the car. "Drive safe, Red."

He slammed the door behind her and strode away.

He didn't even turn to look at her as she drove toward the back entrance. For a crazy second, he thought about not hitting the button on that remote. Not letting her leave.

There would be no excuse for that though. There wasn't a soul for miles. He couldn't keep her here on the pretense of paparazzi when there weren't any to be found.

He'd watched the perimeter fence camera footage for days and there was no one lurking around the property. Whoever Annamae had seen that first day near the fence might really have been a fan or just some local on cleanup patrol of the back road. Besides, Wynn had extra security outside and his contact back in Miami would ensure someone kept an eye on her in Atlanta at least for a few days.

Back inside the farmhouse, he forced himself to watch the security feed as she approached the gate. Waited for it to open. And drove out of his life.

To move on? To face the music? Whatever the hell she called it, the end result was the same. She needed her diva life back in Atlanta. Any hints of a simpler woman beneath the glamor girl had been an illusion.

An acting job.

He pounded his fist on the desk inside the safe room. Pissed off and not knowing where to put it all, he felt the first signs of heartache. He'd cared about her, and she hadn't given a rat's ass about him. That left a mark.

The tiger cat leaped up on the desk, right where he'd just pounded. No wonder the thing got its butt kicked in fights... didn't most felines run at the first sign of trouble? Green eyes stared him down. Fearless even with half an ear.

Wynn gathered the cat up, scratching its neck as he stared at the video monitor showing the back gate. Annamae, the sweetheart of Atlanta cable television, was gone because, according to her, she'd been hiding. While Wynn, a decorated cop professionally trained to take on trouble, continued to sit among his ancient apple trees waiting for his trial date.

Hiding.

To a certain extent, that was a good thing. He'd kept a low profile to stay alive because his testimony was crucial. But with two weeks before the trial, maybe he owed Antony Marks better than just sitting around waiting for his day in court. He could be preparing his statement. Studying the evidence. Moving to a safe house in Miami sooner than the Dimitri family expected so he'd be harder to track...

Setting aside the cat, he pulled another untraceable phone from the bin under the desk and called his contact.

Annamae was right. They couldn't put their head in the sand and hope for the best. There was a time to plan and regroup, yes. But there was also a time to act. And when Annamae had realized that time had come for her, he'd... sure been an ass about it.

When his contact answered, Wynn cleared his throat.

"I'm ready to come in."

An awkward silence followed.

"Already?" his contact said carefully. "You know the

code?"

Wynn reeled off the message that assured he wasn't under duress. Impatient now that he'd made up his mind, he went upstairs and started to put some clothes in a bag. It felt strange thinking about leaving this place where he'd spent so much time. Invested a lot of hard work.

"I'd like the case files sent to the safe house so I can begin my review." He would make sure Antony's voice was heard.

"Sure. Of course. And we'll get you back on the payroll as soon as you're in the city limits." His contact went through a few other details—routine meetings he'd need to attend, Human Resources hoops he'd have to jump through.

He listened with half an ear, his focus on the case. He'd worry about returning to work once he got justice for Antony. Doing right by that kid felt like the most important thing he'd ever done in his career.

Reaching for the alarm clock on the nightstand, he knocked over the book on grafting trees—the one Annamae had been reading. She'd figured out how to coax new life out of dried-up old things faster than him. He shouldn't have held that against her.

"How soon can I expect an escort?" Wynn asked finally, tossing the book in his overnight bag.

"I can have someone there in an hour if that works for you."

An hour? That seemed quick. Maybe his contact was wary about the attention Annamae had stirred up and had placed an escort on standby, just in case.

Could he gather up his life in that amount of time?

Peering around the sparse bedroom, he realized he was already packed. He'd just need to figure out what to do with an army of cats. They'd lived on mice before he arrived, but that hardly seemed fair to consign them to now that they'd known the high life that was Meow Mix.

He'd pay Roofus or Gus or someone to come out to the farm and feed the felines. Check up on them until he figured out what to do with this place.

"An hour works for me." He went still, hearing something outside.

Annamae? It wouldn't be her or the alarm would have gone off.

"Affirmative." His contact disconnected the call.

Wynn went to the window overlooking the carriage house. He didn't see anything. But the hair on the back of his neck rose, an undeniable sense something was off.

He stepped lightly into the hallway. Listened.

A gunshot sounded. Glass shattered somewhere downstairs. Wynn hit the floor.

DID GROWING A backbone require a broken heart?

Annamae felt like hers were closely intertwined as she drove toward the Beulah town line, passing azalea bushes in bloom along a white fence with a sign announcing dates for baseball tryouts at a local park. A lazy day in Beulah, not many people out other than some motorcyclist they'd passed a few miles back.

What she wouldn't have given to take a scenic ride on the back of a bike with her arms around Wynn's waist. To just soak up the sun and the scents of Beulah. Soak up more time with him.

She wished she could have seen more of the town with him while she'd been here. Then again, she wouldn't have minded holing up on the farm with him for weeks on end either. It had taken all her courage to leave a place where she felt genuinely happy.

But was it the place, or was it the man? a little voice in her head asked.

Both, if she was honest. But far more than the man. After all the weeks of questioning herself about Boone and if she loved him enough to marry him, it seemed ironic that she didn't question what she felt for Wynn. Questioned if it was crazy, maybe. But she didn't question if it was real. It was the first real thing in her life in years. And here she was, driving away from him.

She'd fallen for him hard.

"Grandma?" She clutched the steering wheel harder as she slowed for a parade of kids on bicycles, waving home-made flags and dragging stuffed animals in wagons and backpacks.

"Hmm?" Hazel Mae waved to a little boy at the end of the pack. He waved back so hard he forgot to pedal and an annoyed older girl had to yell at him to get moving.

"Do you believe in love at first sight?"

"Thinking about Mr. Lambert without his shirt, aren't you?" her grandmother teased as Annamae continued to head east.

"I just feel bad that I didn't love a guy like Boone who seemed so perfect for me. And yet my surly apple farmer is all kinds of wrong, and yet I felt something strong for him right away."

"First of all, honey, you loved your baseball player. Just not enough to marry him. That's why you worried about that marriage. You knew you hadn't really reached your full potential for caring about someone. They say when it's right, you know. And now you understand what that means, don't you?"

"Did you ever love someone that way?" She glanced sideways. She'd never heard anything about Hazel being married. "Don't answer that if it's too personal."

"I don't mind answering." Her grandmother kept Bagel on her lap for the ride, stroking his ears. "Your grandfather was the love of my life. A fiddle player in a country band who became a big deal in the music business."

"Seriously? My friend Lindsey—the girl whose wedding we're going to attend—her family is in the country music business. Maybe granddad will be at the wedding."

Hazel laughed. "Water under the bridge now! He probably had a girl in every town. But I was his Alabama sweetheart, that's the truth. We both knew when it was time to move on, but I could tell he didn't feel about me the way I did about him. I envied your mother that—my son was as crazy about her as she was about him—but your mama wanted more than love."

"She needed security." Annamae could understand that—kind of.

"You had the option of security, but you didn't take it. You were looking for that big, make-your-heart-beat faster love." Hazel nuzzled the top of Bagel's head. "What I wonder is, did you find it?"

Had she?

Wynn didn't seem like he'd ever been interested in a future with her beyond his trial. But maybe he needed to get through that point in his life as desperately as she needed to set things right back home.

"There's the Sleep Tight Motor Lodge." She pointed out the gas station where Gus Fields worked and she had an idea. "Do you mind if we stop for a minute?"

"Of course not, sweetie. Although don't think I didn't notice how neatly you avoided my question about your feelings for a certain apple farmer." She sent her a knowing look.

Pulling into the gas station lot, she noticed a moped pulling away from the pump, turning onto the street and whizzing away. Just a little bike, but it made her think of the motorcycle she'd passed on the road earlier, her vision blurred then by held-back tears. "There's a parking spot there, dear," Hazel was saying, but Annamae kept staring where the moped puttered down on the county route she'd just turned off. And she scrounged harder through her mind about that motorcycle from earlier. Why did it bother her?

Perhaps because it had been dark, like her mood? Sort of ninja looking, like something out of a movie car chase scene and not what you'd see tooling around a small town at this hour.

Or at all.

And then it hit her. The biker had a backpack with the long handles of a pair of pruning shear sticking out, glinting in the morning sunlight. She'd assumed he was just a local doing some landscaping work ... but now.

"Oh my God." Recognition hit. "That's the guy."

"What guy?" Hazel sat up straighter. "Is he cute?"

Heart racing, Annamae jammed the Beetle into a spot. "A guy who's been watching Wynn. I mean, Heath. That is, I think he wants to hurt him."

She hadn't seen his face, but she knew in her gut that the man on that motorcycle was the one who'd followed her that first day she'd arrived in town. The one who'd been pruning outside Wynn's fence at the orchard. Someone who wanted to silence Wynn before he could testify against a prominent killer. She didn't even stop to wonder why he hadn't made a move sooner or how she was so sure.

She dug in her purse for her cell phone, not caring about locators or tracking. In fact, she needed the world to know her whereabouts this instant. If she were wrong, Wynn would say she was impulsive and rash. If she was right, Wynn could be dead.

"Who are you talking about, Annamae?" Her grandmother sounded lost.

Annamae's brain sped so fast she couldn't act quickly enough to do all the things that needed doing. Fear blasted in her veins. So much adrenaline shot through her she thought she might faint. She felt dizzy. Scared.

But oh God, she needed to save Wynn.

And that thought was enough to steady her thoughts. To spring her into action.

He didn't pick up her call though. She'd memorized the number for one of the pre-paids, but he might not even have it turned on. She'd left without any sure way to get in touch with him.

"Please, Grandma. Take Bagel inside. I need to get help for my apple farmer. I just saw a man who wants to kill him."

And, proving they were absolutely cut from the same cloth, Hazel Mae moved faster than Annamae had ever seen her. She had Bagel in her arms and hurried into the station near the Sleep Tight Motor Lodge just a few steps behind Annamae.

"Mr. Fields!" Annamae waved to Gus where he sat behind the counter with his feet up, watching old Western movies on his iPad. "Please. I need help. Send the police to Heath's farm. There's someone after him, someone who wants him dead. And call the media. Tell them the same thing. Tell them Annamae Jessup said so."

The older man frowned, searching her face. "You sure?"

"Please." Tears burned her eyes. She needed to leave now. "Grandma, call Mom. Tell her to get the story out. *Right now.*"

She tossed the last of her prepaid phones onto the lodge's checkout desk for her grandmother to use. Then, not wasting another precious second, she shoved out the motel doors and raced back to the Beetle.

She would never catch up with that motorcycle. She knew that even as she floored the gas and tore through town. She prayed a cop would chase her and follow her right to the farm, but no one did. When she got to the gate at the back entrance of the farm, the chicken wire and barbed wire had been cut, the barrier drooping open. Alarms were blaring like crazy.

No. No. No.

She could not lose the man she loved this way. She was setting everything to right in her life, not screwing up anymore. Leaving Boone had hurt him and her family. But what if leaving Wynn had cost him his life?

She saw the motorcycle parked in the bushes close to the

farmhouse, but all the rest of the farm remained eerily silent. Terrifyingly so. Jamming the Beetle into park, she prayed the cops would come soon. Or a fleet of paparazzi who would document every moment of this showdown.

Assuming she wasn't too late...

Gut cramping, she sprinted out of the car and filched the pruning shears off the back of the motorcycle as she sprinted past toward Wynn's house.

Should she be running in a zig zag? That's what you did if someone was shooting at you. She knew that from TV, but that was all she knew about bad guys.

That and that they drove ninja motorcycles in the daytime.

Yes, she was hysterical. She had to bite her lip to swallow a crazed laugh as she crept into the house and listened...

Grunts and snarled breathing sounded somewhere in the back of the house.

She fast-walked over broken glass as silently as she could. A cat meowed at her as she passed the kitchen and stepped into the living room.

Wynn was grappling with the intruder on the floor, their hands locked on each other's throats. Their faces red from lack of air and smeared blood—she couldn't tell whose.

Fear and doubt vanished. Certainty gave her strength. Purpose. Clarity.

She hauled back the pruning shears and landed a blow to the biker guy's back. Collapsing him into a heap on the carpet beside Wynn.

"Are you okay?" She tossed aside the garden tool. Shoved at the biker dude's black leather jacket to free Wynn. "Please say you're okay."

His eyes tracked her as she moved. That had to be a good thing. But he didn't sit up yet.

"Better than okay." His voice was hoarse. "I'm one hundred percent good because you're here. Except why are you here?"

Relief flooded through her. Her fingers shook as she touched his face and realized the blood was from a small cut near his eye. Her gaze couldn't roam over him fast enough, checking for damage. Praying he really was safe.

"It's the guy I saw that first day. I saw him driving down the road and later it hit me, I just knew he was heading here. I don't know why today and not earlier … but I knew."

Sirens sounded close by. Very close by.

Jitters were returning now, her brain fuzzy and her nerves buzzing like a low-grade shock. Hell, maybe she was in shock.

"You did great, Red. He was probably going to make his move that first day you arrived but you showed up and things got complicated. More witnesses – or bodies. And once you and your family left, he made his move."

She shivered at how close he'd been to danger and couldn't stop from kissing him. "Thank God you're okay."

"Yeah, about that." He angled his arm behind him and

used it to lever himself to a sitting position.

Only then did she notice he was bleeding profusely from one arm.

"Oh!" Her hand moved toward the wound, but she didn't touch. She'd seen a gun on the floor, but since he'd seemed okay. "You've been shot."

"Just grazed." He turned to keep her from getting too close to the man who'd tried to kill him. "EMTs will fix that right up."

He stroked her hair, his good arm wrapping heavily around her shoulders as she knelt beside him.

"I called the press though." She could hear a helicopter in the distance too, the whoop, whoop of rotors usually the sign of an incoming camera crew from the bigger budget tabloids. "The media are going to be all over this."

"Nice job." His dark eyes locked on hers, a crooked grin preceding a kiss on her cheek. "I like it when you use your powers for good."

"I just wanted anyone here—fast. I thought the press might be quicker than the police."

"No doubt the tabloids have bigger budgets. But I can't meet your fans on my ass. You think you can do me one more favor and help a wounded officer to his feet?"

That hysterical laugh finally did break free. She fought the urge to cover his face with kisses and cry all over him.

"That sounds like the dumbest idea ever for a gunshot victim, but since I'd rather have you lean on me than have you fall while trying on your own… yes."

He leaned heavily on her, but he seemed steady enough as they rose as one.

"Image is everything in this business." His words were a warm caress against her ear as the sirens outside grew louder.

"We were not cut out for this business though, Wynn Rafferty." She spared a glance for the crumpled biker who'd been sent to kill him, but the guy was down for the count.

"That's why we're going to come up with a new plan after we face the music and move on." He turned to face her, toe to toe, his forehead coming to rest on hers.

She breathed in the warmth of him, more grateful than she'd ever felt in her life for a second chance with him.

"I hope that's not an insult." She peered up at him through her lashes.

"That's my way of saying you were right. About everything." He kissed her forehead. "I was hiding here when it was time to move on. Once you left, I knew I wouldn't be staying. I had already called my contact to bring me back to Miami when this guy—"

He shook his head.

"What?"

"The timing seems too perfect close to the trial and just when you left. My contact must have sold me out."

"The press will sniff it out." She felt sure of that much. "It sucks to have them breathing down my neck, but they can be relentless."

"That's a good thing then." He nodded, his weight a bit heavier against her. "They're going to figure something else out."

She glanced up at him. "What would that be?"

He met her gaze, his eyes intense, serious. "That I love you, Annamae."

She held him tighter and soaked up the sincerity in his voice. She couldn't believe she'd almost settled for less than the real thing.

"I love you, too. You're the right one for me," she said with a surety she didn't second guess for even an instant. No doubts. She knew. Even Grandma said so. "I'm not going to run away from this."

"And I'm never going to let you get too far," he promised.

When the police came through the door she called out for an EMT as two officers ran over to secure the biker dude. Wynn found his second wind—or at least enough to fake it through a conversation with a local detective—and he got some medical attention at his kitchen table.

Annamae answered questions, hardly taking her eyes off him the whole time. And even with the house full of cops and emergency responders courtesy of Gus Fields, Annamae could already see her future with Wynn sprawling in front of her. She'd get through the next few weeks back in Atlanta, making things right with her family. Apologizing to a lot of people.

She would miss Lindsey's wedding now, and she regretted that, but she'd do something to make it up to her best friend. She'd saved the man she loved, the man who meant more to her than anyone on earth, and that was the most important thing.

She didn't know for sure what she'd do in Beulah, Alabama with him once he'd put Serge Dimitri behind bars forever, but she could feel her future was right here. In this house where she'd staked everything on love.

The *right* love.

The once-in-a-lifetime love.

Her grandmother had let that kind of relationship slip away from her. Her mother had chosen a different path. But for Annamae, *this* was the happiness she'd dreamed about. She'd found someone who made her feel like the center of his universe. With Wynn, she was the smart one. The pretty one. The One.

And together, they were going to build a rock solid future right here among the cats and apple trees. No more hiding.

"I can hear you thinking over there, Annamae." Wynn said from across the kitchen table as the EMT finished wrapping up his arm.

Threading her fingers with his on the scarred wooden surface, she took strength from that connection before she faced the cameras she knew were waiting outside.

"I'm thinking about how we've got a chance to start over

here. To build any kind of life we want." She didn't care if the EMT could hear.

The awkward sound bite had no power to scare her now that she knew who she was and what she wanted.

"I've got an idea, actually."

"Already?" She grinned at him, grateful she could see his eye better now that the blood on his face had been cleaned up, a neat butterfly bandage in place.

"It's kind of unusual. And crazy."

"Sounds like I'm sure to love it." Her heart ached with happiness. A deep, certain joy that was only going to grow.

And not worrying about the audience, Wynn leaned over the table and kissed her. Once. Twice.

"That's what I love about you. Full of surprises."

By the time the third kiss came, the EMT had declared Wynn well enough and left them alone. Or at least Annamae thought that's what happened. She was too busy falling deeper in love to notice.

Epilogue

One Year Later

THERE HADN'T BEEN any television cameras pointed at her in the apple orchard today. She hadn't needed to consult a radio personality to know if she was making the right decision.

The only person she had needed to consult was herself. And Wynn felt like home.

They had said their vows in the clearing in the orchard, family members circling them. Wynn and Annamae promised to love each other forever right there among the heavy-boughed apple trees. They had decided to write their own vows, a symbol of their commitment to creating a future together.

She smiled as they stepped out onto the dance floor, simple planks brought in and placed outside by the barn. She hadn't wanted a big production. Everything about this day was handpicked from their everyday life. It was real, theirs. The first few notes of their song melted into the air, mixing with the sweet scent of the apple blossoms. Wynn leaned in, placing one hand between her shoulder blades, and took her hand with the other. He traced the lace that formed a v down her back as they danced for the first time as husband and wife.

"You look beautiful, Red," he breathed into her ear as they danced together.

"You clean up pretty nicely too," she teased him, a laugh escaping her lips.

Annamae rested her head against his chest, surveying the gathering of her friends and family.

So much had changed in the past year.

After testifying against Serge, Wynn had decided to honor Antony's legacy. He left the force and established a center for at-risk teens at the farm. While he didn't have much of a green thumb, he did have a knack for nurturing people.

And Annamae's hospitality degree was hard at work. She catered for the center. And for town events as well. Her desserts where near-famous in the surrounding area. That was an accomplishment that was hers alone.

Her eyes fell to her mother and stepfather. They were still the best dressed pair for miles around, but the reality show days were a thing of the past. Spencer had turned his attention back to the sportswear business full time rather than forcing his family back into another season of *Acting Up*. The change suited him, suited them all for that matter, her sisters included.

Hazel Mae's head bopped back and forth to the slow chords. They had grown so close over the past year. Hazel

Mae spent every weekend with Wynn and Annamae, taking up residence in the carriage house. The teens appreciated her spunk and she enjoyed their energy.

Annamae smiled at them, thankful for all that had occurred. And thankful for the chance to meet her biological father. Hazel Mae had arranged their correspondence, and he showered Annamae in postcards from exotic locations.

Her bio-dad stood behind Hazel, dressed in a charcoal suit, hair cut close to his scalp. But he had the look of a wanderer in his eyes, even now. He would be leaving after the reception, still she was glad of his presence all the same. The Smith spirit lived in her, had given her the courage to break away from the mold of expectations. But that decision and capability was always Annamae's for the taking. She realized that now.

When Annamae had walked down the grassy aisle towards Wynn, she'd known that this was the path she was meant to travel. This man and this place were her world. Her joy.

This was *their* story. No script necessary.

THE END

If you enjoyed **The Wedding Audition**, you'll love the next Runaway Bride stories!

THE RUNAWAY BRIDE SERIES

How to Lose a Groom in 10 Days

Book 1: **The Wedding Audition**

Book 2: **There Goes the Bride**

Book 3: **Bride on the Run**

Available now at your favorite online retailer!

ABOUT THE AUTHORS

USA Today bestseller and RITA Award winner, Catherine Mann writes contemporary romance for Berkley, Harlequin, Sourcebooks and Tule. With over sixty books in released in more than twenty countries, she has also celebrated six RITA finals, an RT Reviewer's Award finalist, three Maggie Award of Excellence finals and a Bookseller's Best win. A former theater school director and university instructor, she holds a Master's degree in Theater from UNC-Greensboro and a Bachelor's degree in Fine Arts: Theater (with minors in both English and Education) from the College of Charleston. Catherine and her flyboy husband live on the Florida coast where they brought up their 4 children – and still have 5 four-legged, furry "children" (aka pets). Visit Catherine's website at www.CatherineMann.com

Joanne Rock writes romance of all shapes and sizes from sexy contemporary to medieval historical and an occasional Young Adult story. She's penned over seventy books, appearing most often in the Harlequin Blaze series. Joanne taught English at the college level before becoming a full-time writer, and she returns to the classroom as often as possible to share her love of stories. A quiet and unassuming Virgo, Joanne married a fiery and boisterous Aries man in true opposites-attract fashion. Visit her website at www.JoanneRock.com

Thank you for reading

THE WEDDING AUDITION

If you enjoyed this book, you can find more from all our great authors at TulePublishing.com, or from your favorite online retailer.

TULE
PUBLISHING

CPSIA information can be obtained
at www.ICGtesting.com
Printed in the USA
LVHW042007281118
598532LV00004B/635/P

9 781948 342865